Inspiring
Stories
for Travelers

SOME OTHER STORIES by HARRY KATZAN, JR.

Inspiring Stories for Travelers

HARRY KATZAN JR.

INSPIRING STORIES FOR TRAVELERS

iUniverse books may be ordered through booksellers or by contacting:

iUniverse
1663 Liberty Drive
Bloomington, IN 47403
www.iuniverse.com
844-349-9409

ISBN: 978-1-6632-6535-7 (sc)
ISBN: 978-1-6632-6536-4 (e)

Library of Congress Control Number: 2024915376

Print information available on the last page.

iUniverse rev. date: 07/24/2024

For Margaret, with all my love
now and forever

CONTENTS

Moderate Stories

Longer Stories

INTRODUCTION

This is a book of short stories for travelers. What do you do when riding is a car, plane, or boat, or even staying in a hotel room. What about waiting for a lesson of some kind to be completed. You don't really have enough time to go home and back. You could be waiting for an appointment, or even a cake to bake. If you are deeply in to a good novel, you don't really want to stop reading. If you stop, you have to re-read. Maybe you like to read, but not difficult novels or math books. Perhaps, you would just like to read something different once in a while. Perhaps you would just like to chuckle or say "Oh my." It's also possible that you just don't want to drag some big book around.

We can all read and the modern person is smart through the wonders of evolution. Through modern education, we all know how to use that smartness. A big part of it is reading. Reading is fun, especially if you can enjoy what you are reading.

This book allows you use your brainpower and enjoy it at the same time. But wait. There are times, plenty of them, where you can't read some long complicated stuff, because you have to stop. Then picking up from where you were is not at all possible. Then, why start in the first place. Too often, that is the case.

This book is a collection of 50 short little stories. You can read one in minutes. They are what an alternate read should be: a collection of easy-to-read short stories. Read one then later pick up with another story. They are not related. They are not ordered. You can start at the end and work backward. We call a little story *Story#x*, and they are numbered and the collection is followed by several pages of blank lines on which you can write your thoughts – such as on a story, per se, or someone walking by or sitting next to you.

The price of the book is low, so you can give it to an acquaintance or friend or your spouse or one of your kids. There is no bad language, no sex, and no violence. You can put it on the coffee table or read it on vacation – which is the original intent. You can use it to just take notes. One more thing. The book has been copyrighted but the ideas are free. Use them. I would appreciate the attribution.

Happy reading.

The Author,
June 2024

Harry Katzan Jr.

PART ONE

GETTING STARTED

DESCRIPTION OF THE BOOK

This book is a form of entertainment with a twinge of education along the way.

The collection of stories is not literature in any sense of the word. The objective is simply to entertain you at a time when you aren't able to do anything else. However, there is a little grasp of knowledge in each story. The stories range from being a bit mundane to a touch of genius.

In total, there are fifty stories, so start slowly and finish fast. After reading some of this book, kids, or even older ones, will have a new look on life.

The author's opinion is to start with stories that sound good. The titles are meant to be informative and maybe even humorous. Later, you can graduate to the long jobbies.

Did you ever notice that when you wanted to write something down, you didn't have even a hunk of paper. For that reason, we have some lined paper at the end of the book. It will be good for names, addresses, comments, and perhaps the start of the great American novel. Also complaints about the book.

The stories are categorized into Short Stories, Moderate Stories, and Longer Stories. They reflect not only length, but also content, based on relative importance. There you have it.

Read on and best of luck.

Oh I almost forget. It is a new genre in transportable writing and reading. Don't ask me as to what that means.

PART TWO

THE STORIES

SHORT STORIES

This is a collection of stories that are short
In length and are easy to read.
They should get you started in
A world wind of ideas

How to Succeed in Business

One of my friends was interested in how to succeed in business. Countless books have been written on the subject. One of the best is a small book written by a Harvard MBA by the name of Jeffrey J. Fox with the title How to Become CEO. Here are five simple ideas:

Always remember your subordinates' spouses.

Don't go over budget.

Never underestimate an opponent.

Please, be polite with everyone.

Eat breakfast in your hotel room.

In the book, there are seventy-five of such ideas.

Someone asked Onassis, the wealthy and successful business man, who married Jacqueline Kennedy. Supposedly, he was to have said, "Have a good suntan, have a firm handshake, and wear good shoes." It probably isn't exactly true, but it sounds good.

The suntan is worthy of a few words. Without question, a person looks better when they have a good suntan for business, social occasions, and just plain living. But, I think we should a little farther with the suntan business.

What does a person do when they are getting a suntan? It is calm. There are no business distractions. You can think better, and make better decisions and come up with better ideas.

By the way, do you know what is Onassis' first name is. It is Aristotle. We go by the last name.

Do you know what the great philosopher Aristotle's last name is also Onassis. In those days they went by the first name.

Just thought you might be interested.

A Good Student

My wife and I know a couple with four kids and a really strict demeanor. From day one, the kids were taught to talk properly at home, and outside of the home. They dressed nicely and seemed to know more about things than most kids. For example when the boys in the neighborhood were to go somewhere, they always met at their house. The mother checked out their shoes and applied shoe polish whenever necessary. When the mother and her kids went somewhere, they had to walk, eat, and talk like adults. The oldest boy, in particular, was a whiz in his studies in grammar school. Whenever the teacher wanted to demonstrate something, she would call on him. His nickname was Sonny. On one occasion when no one in the class could name the 8 reindeers in Christmas tradition, Sonny rattled off Dasher, Dancer, Prancer, and Vixen, Comet, Cupid, Donner, and Blitzen without a pause. His teacher, Mrs. Zalibek, was amazed. All of the other teachers were likewise impressed with Sonny's academic progress.

On the journey home on one afternoon, Sonny entered a crosswalk when the crossing guard was holding up the stop sign. A lady ran through the sign and hit Sonny, breaking his right leg.

At St. Luke's Hospital, the doctors were worried. They could fix Sonny's right leg all right, but while the leg was mending, the left leg would continue growing. They decided on a dual full leg cast with a bar in between for stability. Sonny was destined to be at home for at least six weeks.

When Mrs. Zalibek visited her favorite student at the hospital, she heard the devastating news. Sonny was 7 years old, a critical time in his intellectual development. No solution seemed to be available. But it was.

Mrs. Zalibek was an unusual person. Every day, after school for 6 weeks, she visited Sonny at his home, talked to him, and delivered his lesson plan to Sonny's mother for the day. Sonny didn't miss a single day of his education and turned to be an excellent husband, good father, gentleman, professor, author, and marathon runner, all of which was enabled by a fine teacher.

Thanks Mrs. Zalibek.

How the System Works

This is an anecdote about a young boy picking beans and strawberries to earn money in order to go to college. It is not me, but I am using the first person because Steve suggested we do so. By the way, a short little story is sometimes called an anecdote if it's really short.

Somehow and somewhere I got the notion that I wanted to go to college. I was in grammar school. It could be Mrs. Zalibek's student in Read #5. He might be me in this anecdote. We are using the first person as you know.

The anecdote revolves around a farmer that stopped at the corner of our street to pick up boys to pick beans and sometimes strawberries on his farm. He paid by the pint that is two cups. To many kids, it was like a day of fun. To me, it was serious business.

When we got from our street to the farm, I was the first to take off his shirt to get a suntan and immediately started to pick beans. We picked a pint of beans and took them to the farmer's son who kept count for each kid. I picked beans furiously from the start of the picking until noon, at which time we had our lunch that our mother had packed for us. Usually it was a bologna or peanut butter sandwich. Water was free from a well on the farm. By noon, most of the boys were already complaining how hot it was and all of that. Some already stopped and were sitting under a tree. Not me. I picked furiously until quitting and payroll time about 5 o'clock.

Then the fun began. The farmer would say your name and his son would give the number of pints picked. Normally, it was 20 or 25 and the farmer paid on the spot.

Finally, the farmer came to me and I always waited until last. The farmer's son would read off a much higher number like 40. The farmer would say, "Give him 50." The farmer liked me because I was serious and didn't waste his time. I had learned the system.

The anecdote is not finished. I had a bankbook because that is what they used in those days. I would go to the bank window to deposit a small amount of money, and some employee would say with a smirk in his voice, "What are you going to do with all of that money." I always said, "I'm going to college." I'm sure that I got the last laugh, as they say.

STORY #4

The B-52 Apron

When I was just out of college at my first position with a aerospace company in the northwest, I was amazed at the enormity of the operation. After the first day, I was enrolled in airplane school in which we were familiarized with the complicated process of putting an aircraft together. The notion of flight was presented along with airplane wings, positive loading, and all of the basic components, and where they were manufactured or outsourced to another company in another country. We learned about wind tunnels, assembly, and the overall process. We were shown all of the buildings and how they camouflaged during World War II. During the war, they were turning out 16 bombers a day, but when I got there it was one every once in a while. How long it took to make a bomber was a secret.

The size of a B-52 is beyond belief. It has a wingspan of 185 feet and a height of 40.7 feet. It has 8 jet engines mounted in 4 twin pods. The maximum speed is 595 miles per hour at 50,000 feet. It has a payload of 70,000 pounds and can carry a lot of bombs. During flight, the wings can move up and down 17 feet. It has a crew of 7. It is almost 4 stories. high It is a large and impressive airplane.

When the B-52 is finally assembled, it is moved out into an apron in front of the assembly building and next to the four lane highway. The air field is across the highway and has a flight center for operations. At that time, there were military jet fighters that were used as chase planes. No one knew exactly what the chase plans did, other than take pictures.

If there was a B-52 sitting on the apron when I left for home after work, I knew that the plane was complete and would be moved across the highway to the air field during the night. They would stop traffic in both directions, take down the fences, and move the large plane across.

I knew the plane would take off the next morning and be flown to an Air Force air base.

So, I left for work early to watch the takeoff event. I was using the Burroughs E101 computer, programmed with pins, and it was in the flight center for some unknown reason. I wanted to be finished with my work and no on minded if you came in early. Coming in late, on the other hand, was to be avoided. When the B-52 was about to take off, the jet pilots would take off. Since there were no Air Force officers around and they had their fun, frequently using their afterburners. The B-52 would taxi down the takeoff lane and fly to the air base it was slotted for, never to be seen again. Everything was a big secret. It was a sight to behold, that was never to be forgotten.

Charlotte Airport

This is a short little read. But it is kind of interesting because it gives an example of how things evolve in the modern world. I am the individual involved. It takes place when I was a student in a summer job. It was in Charlotte, North Carolina. I was hired to manage a project to redraw the mechanical drawings for the Redstone and Jupiter missiles. I had to hire a team of young people who knew how to do engineering drawing. When engineering changes are made, the drawings have to be updated. It was early in the space and missile era, so there were a lot of changes. They were just penciled in on the originals.

The information was not secret from the governmental point of view but employees had to have a good background. To get a confidential clearance, and all you needed was a good credit rating. That was easy. Just call Fort Belvoir, an Army installation, and they did it for you. Next, I had to learn to do engineering drawing. That was accomplished in an evening's reading. All we had was to redraw the drawings and the project was completed.

There was more to the position. It contracted with a company that makes oil filters to reorganize the manner in which it did their work. We used the method of least squares to predict future sales. Now they call the method regression. The company did not believe our prediction of the future sales but our prediction was right on the button.

There is, however, another reason why I am giving this read to you today. The company started from humble beginnings during

World War II. The first owner, to put it neatly, was just old and tired. He sold the engineering and architecture firm to the current owner for an amount to be paid out in future earnings. No money was exchanged at the time of purchase, but paid out in several months. The reason I am telling you about this company is that the new owner had no education past the third grade. He learned engineering through self-study in the evenings. This is absolutely true, believe it or not.

What did they do to gain such a high reputation. They got a contract to do the architectural and engineering design of the building to build the Nike Hercules Missile used for a large-scale defense. The Nike Ajax, a small missile, was good for small targets but not strong enough to bring down big enemy bombers. The Nike Hercules was designed as a major upgrade. The building was built and then the U.S. Defense Department cancelled the contract for the Hercules. The defense need was satisfied by another defense missile. The question is, what happened to the beautiful building? It is now the Charlotte Airport, one of the most classy airports in the United States.

Now you know the end of the story.

Wrestling Championship

Every year there is a state wrestling championship. There are several weight categories for student athletes ranging from about 116 pounds to heavy-weight of 180 pounds or more. Our school had last year's champion in the heavy weight class. He wrestled, played football, and lifted weights for conditioning; he looked like Mr. America. His father was very successful in home building and they had a weight room at home. He was smart too and was a member of the National Honor Society. The state championship was to be held across town in a large high school with an enormous seating arrangement for spectators.

Allen, Bill, Charles, and Dan were members of the track team and had been schoolmates since kindergarten. They knew each other and liked each other. Charles was a black fellow and the rest were Caucasian. The four of them thought that it would be enjoyable to watch their schoolmate win the state championship once again. They decided to meet at the streetcar turnaround at W. 140th Street at 6:00, and that would give them time to cross the city to the high school where the championship was to be held. Dan said, "I can borrow my mom's car and we can leave at 7:00. That gives us some extra time." They all agreed.

On the day of the championship at 6:30, Bill called Allen and said that they weren't going. Allen thought, 'Our transportation is gone. Maybe Charles doesn't know so I should go to the station.' On the way to the station, Charles called from afar, "Is that you

Allen?" When Allen finally got to the station, he said, "The dirty rats. We know what is going on." Allen and Charles decided to take the streetcar and travel across town.

They had an enjoyable time. Nothing better, but they were too late for the heavyweight match. But, their schoolmate won. They were happy, and they enjoyed the streetcar ride back home. They never talked to Bill and Dan again. They were, indeed, dirty rats.

At a football practice, sometime later, Allen, who was a lightweight, was told to block against the heavyweight champion who ran through Allen like he wasn't there. The football coach was mad, not angry, but realmad. All Allen said when he got up from the turf, "What did you expect?" The other football players just looked at the coach like he was an idiot. He sure lost some points that day.

Did the heavyweight champion go to College? He sure didn't. After graduation, he went into the building business with his father. It takes all kinds to make a world.

Life Capsule

Hello, my name is George Small. I have an interesting little story. Actually, many of you guys might call it an anecdote, which is what some people call a little short story. I worked for the Lehman Company that make all of those missiles and airplanes. I needed to know more about business and economics in order to get the kind of position I wanted. I was an engineer and left to get an MBA, which was the custom in those days for engineers. I attended a major university and obtained a good background in business and other things. Then I returned and the HR department of Lehman that arranged several interviews for me to obtain a suitable position.

There were several options: marketing, advanced engineering on new products, computer science, finance, and one new secret project. They felt that I was suitable for it because of my diverse background. It was the life capsule, known by some people as the biosphere.

Remember this was during the cold war that most persons were well aware of. In the event of a serious nuclear attack, there were two major subjects. One is to cure persons that were exposed to atomic radiation, and the second is prevent persons from being exposed in the first place.

For the first problem, the government developed the well know bone marrow transplant, that was being developed in major government sponsored research laboratories. The second was to develop a biosphere in which people could live. In was in the research stage. This read is about the latter.

Lehman was charged with experiment with testing the technology. The project was involved with four subjects – all related. The first was the container in which people would live. The second, third, and fourth were what was in the container to be effective. The person was the experimental subject. The second was one or more carp fish, the third, was an effective collection of plants, and of course there was water to help the third do the job of helping the person stay alive. Of course, there were a lot of plans and experiments to make the system work.

I chose computer science, because it appeared to have the most promising future, and if course that was the best choice.

I never found out what happened to the *Life Capsule.* There was a rumor it was transferred to another location, perhaps Area 51, but you never know.

Harry Katzan Jr.

Running in the Hallway

I went to high school in the city. It was a large school and there were pretty many rules, two of which were the up and down procedures for the stairways, and the rule that there was absolutely no running in the hallways. The halls were wide with student's lockers on both sides. The majority of students planned to go to college and that turned out to be true. Behavior was refined for high school. That is, until I came along.

For some reason that I can't seem to remember, at the moment, I ran down the stairs and on down the crowded hallway. That is, until I met an obstacle. A teacher who happen to be on hallway duty. She was a small female gym teacher. She wasn't just angry, she was mad, real mad. She grabbed me by the front of my shirt and slammed my head up against a steel locker. No once, but 6 times. The hallway was quite crowded and the students, especially the girls were aghast. I heard one of the girls say, "She's in real trouble." The teacher, Mrs. Johnson, said, "Why are you running?" All I managed to say was, "I'm sorry Mrs. Johnson, I won't do it again. I promise." The back of my head hurt like the dickens. I didn't exactly know why I was running in the crowded hallway, but I was.

Mrs. Johnson was a small person and just over did it. The students said she was sure to get fired. When I got home that afternoon, my mother asked what had happened to my bloody head. All I said was that I fell playing football; but it wasn't football season. She had four kids and did not have time for small details. I never told my mother or father what had happened.

During the next few days, I saw Mrs. Johnson in the hallway and she was meek and mild. Probably afraid that I would tell the principal. I never said a word to anyone. Not my friends and not my not-friends. After a week or two, Mrs. Johnson realized that nothing was going to happen, and she softened up.

When I graduated at the end of that school year, she wrote a nice message in my graduation book. I learned my lesson, and also that there are times when silence in the best solution.

Blocked Funds

I have this colleague who has written a few books on computers, one of which was one on a subject called Operating Systems. It was a popular subject. A few months after the book's publication, he happened to come to the faculty lunch table with a copy of that book that had been translated into Russian. A grandiose conversation took place about the Russians stealing books. One of our colleagues was a professor whose teaching specialty was Russian Economics. The author happened to mention that he wouldn't get any royalties, but it was nice to have a couple of copies in Russian. He was kind of proud about it.

The academic specialist in Russian economics was quick to mention that wasn't so. The Russians do not steal. They make one big publication and store them in a huge warehouse. They keep track of the number of copies sold and the author has a money account in a Russian bank. They are known as Blocked Funds. If you go to Russia, you can get them.

Funny thing. The same author wrote a book on IBM computers. The book was used in a graduate class in computer organization. One of the students from Iran just happened to mention to the professor that that he was translating his book to Farsi. The professor replied, "Why are you translating the book into Farsi, when you can read it in English." The Iranian student did not answer.

Subsequently, there were news items covering the stealing of IBM computers, perhaps the smaller models, and how prevalent it was. They were taken right out of companies that needed them for everyday operations. The incident took place in several European and Middle Eastern countries. But the article mentioned that is some countries, IBM reference manuals were not printed in their native language, and had to be translated into their language.

In that vary professor's courses, computers were used for everyday instruction. There was a computer on each student's desk. Away for an international conference, he found that 4 computers were stolen from the last row of the classroom that he used. The university had excellent security facilities, but somehow they were gone, and they were missing after the penultimate weekend. They were not reported to the administration because the Asian professors were afraid the they would be blamed for stealing them. Then to top it off, the computers were replaced and then stolen again in the succeeding week, in spite of the fact that were bolted to the desks. The computers were then replaced and bolted and chained to the desks and the problem was solved.

And that is the end of this caper.

Run, Run, Run

It was balmy spring evening when my friend across the street and I decided we should be getting in shape for the upcoming baseball season. We were 12 or 13 years old, I can't exactly remember. I had a typical home life after dinner: rinse the dishes, then wash and dry them, and put them away. My friend Bob essentially had the same routine.

It was a nice neighborhood in the late 40s or 50s. All or most of the men were employed in 9 to 5 jobs, and the mothers stayed at home. All of the families had a car and most men took public transportation, such as a street car or a bus. Traffic was light on our street, that was sandwiched between two churches. To the best of my knowledge, none of the families had much money, but none were poor. After dinner – some people called it supper – the kids were free to do whatever they wanted. But without much money, no one could do much, except go up to the corner to see what was going on. If you had an extra dime, you could go up to the corner drug store and have a cherry phosphate and a little bag of Fritos.

So Bob and decided to take a little run. We ran side-by-side down the middle of the street down to the corner and around and half-up the next street and return. Maybe it was at half mile and maybe it wasn't. Speed or distance was not of concern. It was fun. After 2 or 3 evenings, our younger brothers tagged on behind. Then some other kids on the street added themselves on our runs. The traffic was light; we were on a side street in the city. There were plenty of kids. In fact, enough for two baseball teams. The number of boys that were running grew rapidly until some of the neighbors came out to watch. Then 2 or 3 older girls asked if they could run with us. They were probably about 14 or 15. Of course, we said more the marrier. Then some parents asked if their little kids could run with us. Speed was not of the essence. Some of the parents even ran with their little kids.

We even had a name. ***Run Run Run***.

We continued with Run Run Run for 5 days a week until school started in September. And then, we never started again,. We never knew why.

The Wrong House

One of the pleasures of growing up in the United States is that there is a good chance you will have a good friend to do things with. Boys usually call them their buddy. Essentially, it is just a couple of boys that do things together. If you have a bunch of kids in a neighborhood, they talk and hang out together. Kids know everything. Good or bad. Right or wrong. When they faced adversity, they faced it together. When you see two buddies headed for the corner to find out what is going on, you can assume they are talking about a subject important to one of them. If you have a buddy, you experience life together.

Since buddies experience life together, and if one of them has a problem, it is useful to talk to your buddy. We talked about good things and things that were not so good. When, I grew up, we had to experience the prospective of military conscription, also known as the draft. Many boys trained together to better condition themselves for military service.

My buddy, who I call Jimmy whose proper name is James, and I did most things together. I had met Jimmy's father but did not have any experience with him. The same with my father. His father went every Thursday to some club – could be a church – where they drank alcoholic beverages, and came home, as they called it, blasted. My father, on the other hand, went fishing with our next door neighbor and where I participated. I was a good fishing person.

Jimmy's father loved hunting and was a crack shot. My father played sandlot baseball well into his forties.

Our backgrounds were different but we were buddies. Jimmy got a driving learner permit, and I waiting to take driver ed in high school. Once, Jimmy on a trip for baseball supplies, crashed into the Giant Tiger building with their 1933 Chevy. They only lived 4 doors down the street, but I didn't go over there because I thought the father would be very angry. He wasn't.

Now here is the story. Jimmy and his older brother were painting a bright green border around their front door. Apparently, their father went to the wrong home when coming home on Thursday, every Thursday. Too much booze. Finally, our little world erupted. Jimmy's father come home, as they said intoxicated, and when his wife confronted him, he hit her in the mouth and broke a tooth. Things had to change in their family. Someone, a preacher, priest, teacher - I never knew – told the family that every time the father went for a drink, put a Pepsi in his hand. This resulted in multiple trips of Jimmy and I to the store on the corner to bring back two cases of Pepsi. We use a little red wagon from their childhood. The father was apparently cured of too much drinking. Later, we discovered that it was likely that the father had dementia and perhaps other cognitive disease, and not alcohol, that cause the problem. So, you never know.

Talking in Math Class

You never know how things are going to turn out. This an example out of a simple math class – algebra to be exact. The story involves two boys and their involvement in class behavior.

The teacher was really excellent. She was patient and presented the subject matter clearly and distinctly. She usually repeated a subject at least twice. There was a problem, however, and that was because off me and the student sitting behind me, named Eric. We were either smart in math, the subject was easy, or both, which was probably the case.

Now the teacher – let's call her *Teach* for the time being - preferred strict discipline. No talking, no moving around, and making sure to hand in your homework in strict compliance with her rules. But mostly, teach did not like students talking in class unless they were asked to. Period.

The situation started during the first week of class. Teach covered some absolutely simple topic. Oh, by the way I am Allen, not in real life but in this read. Then teach repeated it for students that were not paying attention and Allen said a few words to Eric and Teach gave him that look. Allen kept on talking, and Teach asked him a question about the topic just covered, and the class gave a look. Allen answered correctly without batting an eye.

The next day, Teach covered and repeated a harder topic. Allen started up again talking with Eric and this time Eric responded to Allen is hushed tones. Teach asked a question, and again Allen responded with the correct answer.

The scenario was repeated more than several times in the next few weeks and Allen responded correctly in each and every case. It was time for the first exam, and Teach was astounded that the overall class grade with better than ever in her 30 year career teaching math.

The Principal called Teach into his office and congratulated her on her success. Then he told her what had happened. He, the Principal, was Allen's uncle and the entire scenario was planned from the start. The rest of the class was competing with Allen and Eric, and that aided their learning of mathematics.

Now you know the while story.

The Neighborhood

What is a neighborhood? Most of us live in a neighborhood, but it seems that many of us has never thought of what one is. It is a community within a town or city in which people interact which each other. The people in a neighborhood are known as neighbors. A neighborhood refers to a place, and a neighbor is a person. Got it?

Neighbors usually interact with one another and have something in common, although that statement should be regarded with some trepidation. Sometimes communities are formed when a builder builds a collection of homes Neighborhoods are frequently based on ethnic backgrounds when people emigrate from the same source.

Our neighborhood, at that time, was built just after the depression in 1935. As I was growing up, we went through various stages. We always had heat and electricity, even though some homes had coal furnaces. But, then we went through refrigerators, washers and driers, sewing machines, telephones, TV, and other things. When not everyone had a fridge, we had an ice man who came on a horse drawn carriage and threw chunks of ice to the kids. Also, the junk man came around with a horse drawn carriage. The milk man came around every morning.

No one squealed to the city if something was improper except the time when it was discovered that a home up near the corner had an outhouse, and I 'm not sure they had running water. The telephone lines must have been busy on that day, even when we still had party lines shared by a bunch of families. Another strange thing was the house on the next street. Up to the time I went to college when I was 18, there was a horse in their vacant lot on that street RIGHT IN THE MIDDLE OF THE CITY.

We played softball in the street in front of our house. The manhole cover was home plate and the sewer drains were the bases. The ladies across the street called the cops who always responded to see what we were doing. You would think we would run and we did; right up to the police car to see what they wanted. They took our names and gave us a lecture and we gave our real names. We liked the cops and weren't afraid to give our real names. As they drove away, they threw the crumpled list of names out of the car window. There was a city ball field with 6 diamonds at the end of our street – about 300 yards. We preferred the street. Actually, if the ladies across the street gave good Halloween candy or even money, we were nice about it and moved a ways down the street.

We even played touch football in the street. The manhole covers were the goal lines and the curbs were the side lines. There is more later on the sports read.

Running

Running. Of all things, what exactly is running? Is fast jogging running? What is jogging? Is fast walking jogging? Oh my goodness, what is Walking? It seems like we have a long way to go with the original question. It is propelling one's self when your both feet are off the ground. Even horses run when they gallop.

They say that running is good for you. I don't know who came up with that crazy idea. It seems to be appropriate when you are in danger or playing a sport like football, baseball, basketball, and soccer. Even with some other sports like tennis, you don't actually run. In the read titled Run Run Run, kids ran after dinner but that was a special case.

I met this guy that ran over 800 races and almost 100 marathons. He has over 500 t-shirts and I wonder what he did with all those trophies and awards. To top it off, he used those log books and accumulated over 46 thousand miles. All he got out of it was two worn out knees that had to be replaced. He could not run anymore, so he stopped and never looked back. Now walking, that's a good idea. In Germany, they have these 'volk laufs' – that means peoples walk – where a lot of people walk about 25 miles at their own pace. If they finish, they get one of those awards that you can sew onto your jacket.

My wife and I were in Switzerland where I ran a 12 mile race that was off road. It was my first race ever. We were waiting for the race and some guy had pulled himself a pint and was drinking.

Someone said that the race was ready to start, He chug-a-lugged his beer and took off running. I never saw him in the race because he was so far ahead. When I got home, I had to take a nap.

Once when I was working in Boston, there was a race in New Hampshire. So after work, my wife and I drove up and stayed overnight. The race started in the morning. In every race, there was this guy who threw up at about the one mile mark. It happened at least 3 times that I witnessed. Probably, his mother said, "Eat plenty, you're belly is big" for breakfast.

One day when we were in New Hampshire again, I went out for my morning run and got chased by a pig. True. She was behind me. When I stopped, she stopped. This went on for about a mile. Some high school kids, playing hooky grabbed the pig and did something with her. I wish I had a camera.

If you don't like this read, please put that in your Comments and Notes. I'll look for it.

Being Followed

I have what I think is a good example of how things work in the real world. When you work on a government contract or are an outsourcer on major project, it possible to have contract cancellations and employee layoffs. That is easy to say, but how is it really done, so as to have a stable workforce. It is not so simple.

If you lay off only workers then when a new contract is received, you have no one to do the work. If you lay off only managers, then you have no one to guide the workers. So what is an equitable solution to this problem?

You have a totem pole and an employee's position on the totem pole is determined by education, experience, age, evaluation, and so forth. I was high on the totem pole, and my position was even higher than my immediate manager. I could do things that others could not,

On one very busy morning, traffic on an overpass was blocked up and I got a flat tire. What to do?. I had never changed a tire before. The man in the car behind me jumped out of his car to assist. He was nicely dressed but not too fancy. He said, "I'll take care of it for you," and he did. I remember saying, "Can I give you something?" He said no, it was his job, and I remembered that. I was quite young and regarded it as a bit of good luck.

When I got to work late, I told my manager that I had a flat tire and he said, "I know." And that was it. Only later did I realize that I was being tailed by a security person to safeguard employees high on the totem pole from any kind of misfortune. Good employees were valuable.

Government contracts were strict and equipment was necessary and if something were one day late, they would be fined a million dollars. Of course, the money in the contracts was huge. There is more to the story.

Many of the assemblies are outsourced to other firms and countries. They could have problems. That is the way it is. Accordingly, every single part on an aircraft, for example, could be built in-house by an enormous manufacturing facility. It was perhaps a little less efficient than buying subcontracted parts, but they could be built in-house to meet a deadline. People in that category are often valuable.

And that is the end of a long story.

Cigarettes

Most of us were not even born during World War II. The country was not exactly in the war, but our production capability more than helped win the war. And the amount of men and boys killed in that terrible war was beyond belief. The number of lives that were changed if not ruined was very high.

Jobs were plentiful and the economy was strong. The country was going into debt for the first time. Buying war bonds was a patriotic thing to do and many families had victory gardens. Gasoline was in short supply and it was rationed. My father, for example, received gasoline stamps but rode the streetcar to work. We then had gas for a Sunday drive to get honey ice cream, because sugar was rationed. Cars were not being built. The car factories were converted to building planes, tanks, and guns. One big plant near our home was producing 16 bombers per day. Cars were simple and most men had tool kits in the trunks of their cars and could fix the cars that broke down, right on the road.

Anyone who wanted to work could get a good paying job, for the first time in the world's history. Cigarettes were not rationed but they were scarce because the was a pack of Lucky Strikes in every K-ration kit along with a chocolate bar.

One of the items that was not rationed but in short supply were cigarettes. That was mentioned previously. They were distributed through the grocery stores. The notion of a supermarket was not yet in vogue. The woman when paying for their food would ask the cashier if she had any cigarettes, and they would customarily get a no. The cashier was an enormous woman who was the laughing stock of the neighborhood. Her name was Frieda. The kids would laugh and say that she could never get a husband. About then there was a guy in the neighborhood that was as skinny as he possibly could be and more than a bit ugly to boot. His name was Roger, and he was 4-F. The neighborhood kids all called him 'Mister 6-F'. The kids laughed and said that when Roger went through the checkout line, Frieda would have cigarettes. And, she did. A short time later, they were married.

There is always an easy way to solve a problem.

How to Play Polo

One of the oldest matches in world history is the *Polo Match*. It originated in ancient England and is still played there. It involves men, horses, polo clubs, helmets, and a little ball. The objective is the hit the little ball into the opponent's goal.

The match is as much a ceremony as it is a game of physical prowess. The teams eat together and compete together. All polo matches are not the same in the manner it is played and the size of the playing field.

The match consists of two four-man teams and 24 horses. The horses are trained to play the polo game by running after the ball. The players use a polo club to hit the ball. The way the match is set up, the player must hit the ball with his club in his right hand. If a player is not right handed, he must still use the club on the right hand side of the horse.

The principle of a polo match is very similar to ice or field hockey. The polo players learn to play together, by passing the ball and performing special procedures.

A game consists of six periods called a chukka. Each chukka last as 7 ½ minute periods. The horses are changed after the end of each chukka periods. The size of a nominal polo playing field is 300 yards long and 160 yards wide.

Polo matches are 2 hours long and there is no stopping in the match for any reason. Doctors are typically present and players are sometimes injured. The helmets are a necessary accessory since players are frequently knocked from their horses.

Typical royals in England participate in horse-back riding with jumping, hunting, fishing, and polo. The game is so rough that it is no wonder that it is not played in other countries. In some sense of the word, it is analogous in flavor to rugby, a form of football.

Intelligence

People are always talking about intelligence, but what in the devil is it? Many people think that intelligence is what an intelligence test measures. But that is certainly no definition. Some essential qualities of intelligence might be the following:

- Respond to situations very flexibly
- Take advantage of fortuitious circumstances
- Made sense out of ambiguous or contradictory input
- Recognize the relative importance of different elements of a situation
- Find similarities between situations despite differences that may separate them
- Draw distinctions between situations despite similarities which may link them
- Synthesize new concepts by taking old concepts and putting them together in new ways
- Come up with ideas that are novel

Viewed in this manner, intelligence is a form of computation. Effective intelligence then is a process and an appropriate machine in which to execute the process. Well, that is perhaps a good start but what about some examples.

There are two things that will spur your interest in intellegence that are facinating in there own right. The Turing test and a computer program named ELIZA.

Alan Turing is an English mathematician whose work on cryptography was a major contribution to the victory in World War II. Almost single handedly, he developed a machine that could solve the German's cryptographic enigma code that was used to win the war for the allies. He is also very well known for the development of basic concepts in mathematics and computation.

Dr. Turing is best known for a variety of intellectual concepts, but the most well known is the Turing Test for artificial intelligence. The fundamental idea is based on the idea that a computer exhibits intelligence when it can answer questions, and a person can or cannot tell that it is a computer answering the questions. The basic result is that if a computer is mistaken for a human more than 30% of time during a set of keyboard interactions, then it is exhibiting intelligence. The test works as follows. There are three computers connected together and two people and one supposedly intelligent program. One person asks the questions and the other two computers answer the question. If the program can answer the questions and it is undetectable that is a the computer, then that program exhibits intelligence. Turing also gives conditions for conducting the "Turing test," but that is the basic idea behind the test."

"There is another AI-type program named ELIZA developed by Joseph Weizenbaum at MIT in 1966. The on-line program uses the input to determine the response, as in non-directive counseling in Psychology. ELIZA is on-line and here is no secret about how it operates. Yet, so many people begin to believe it, that many universities - including MIT - had to take it offline.

Harry Katzan Jr.

The user person just says things to ELIZA and ELIZA responds just like an ordinary person would, using the information in the person's input. The ELIZA program is not that simple. It has to stay on the beam, so to speak. Most people don't think of that when they think of Artificial Intelligence, but it would seem to have intelligence.

There is no doubt about it, intelligence is an up and coming subject.

MODERATE STORIES

This is a group of stories that are a
Little longer in length
And perhaps a little more
Complicated

The Survivorship Bias

This is a story about a military officer who jump-started his career by solving a knotty problem for the Army Air Force during World War II.

It involves two First Lieutenants in the Army Air Force, who completed their required number of 25 missions as P-51 support pilots that accompanied B-17 bomber runs in World War II. Most fighter pilots were shot down before they could complete their required number of missions. The two lieutenants were ordered to report to the commander and received their promotions to Captain, given two weeks leave, and ordered to report to the Pentagon for duty or assignment. The two pilots enjoyed their two weeks leave in New York City, along with a fine hotel and good food

At the Pentagon, the brand new Captains were ordered to report to a high level secret meeting concerning the number of P-51 airplanes that were shot down in a single mission, which was roughly 60%. The commanders of the U.S. and Britain believe that a failure rate that high could not be sustained in terms of personnel and equipment.

The Air Force tried titanium panels as armament and the method did not work. So, the big guns were brought in to solve the problem. The meeting was being attended by three-star generals, college professors, and noted scientists. The problem was well defined. All of the bullet holes were covered up but the planes continue to be shot down. The Captain, who the story is all about, said "I can solve the problem." The other Captain said "Are you out of your mind? You're probably going to get us demoted."

The first Captain replied, "Don't worry, I'll solve the problem."

The Captain was asked to describe the method that he said would solve the problem. Here is his response. "The objective of the meeting is to determine where titanium plates are to be placed for protection of P-51s. Here are some photos." The photos showed P-51s with bullet holes. "The planes have been plated where the holes are with no improvement. Now, that is the reason why we are here. It's an easy problem." The Captain calmly continued, "It's easy gentlemen. The important holes went down with the plane – in fact, probably caused it. Look at the photos, do you see any planes with holes in the bellies, for example. We should plating areas where there is no holes. If the Army Air Force would armor plate the untouched areas evident in the photos we have, the problem will be solved," said then Captain.

The armor plating was placed in clean aircraft bellies, and the percent of shot down planes was reduced to 10%. The two Captains were promoted forthwith to the rank of Major. The mathematician who described the method named it *survivorship bias*

I Would Never Call the Cops

We used to live in New Hampshire. Now New Hampshire is a very beautiful state in which to live. The people are nice – except when they are not – the housing is reasonable, and there is no tax on earned income. The winters are cold and there is a mountain to run or walk up. Oh, I forgot that there is a lot of skiing. Lots of it.

The newspapers are helpful and people read them. On this occasion, there was an announcement to the effect that if you saw a racoon in the daylight, be careful and call the police. The critter is rabid because it is a nocturnal animal.

On this day, my wife looked out of the back window and swears that she saw a racoon. I mean a rabid racoon. Being a person with all of those nice attributes, I called the police and in twenty minutes or so, up the driveway came the police car. The officer was nice. Everyone is nice in New Hampshire. I said that already. He asked what was the matter, and I said that my wife had seen a rabid racoon and he had run into the woods to the side of our house. We had a big yard - all 13 acres of it. He was wearing a police special suspended on his right side, ready for a quick draw.

So what did the magnificent officer of the law do, he went to his ankle and pulled out a baretta. Just like the movies. In a little while, he came out with nothing in hand. I hadn't heard a shot or anything, but you never know, they might have a silent guns now-a-days. Times change things.

When I asked what he had found, he said it was a mother fox and her babies. He looked disgusted, and went to his car, said something on his radio, and left in a hurry.

Within two minutes, the farmer next door came wheeling up the driveway and jumped out of his car. That's two in one day. A world's record. Did you call the police on me, he asked excitedly. Calm old me said that I had called the police for a rabid racoon that turned out to be a nursing mother fox. Never, I said, would I ever call the police on another person.

The next door farmer was happy, because it was against the law to shoot inside of the town. He had been trying to get rid of weasels, or whatever they are – I'm a city boy – and they churn up the ground so he couldn't plant his plants. Pardon the good English, I studied Math and not English.

But, that is not the end of the story. Within 30 minutes, my wife came and said I should look out the side window. Oh, I thought. Another rabid racoon. But, it wasn't. It was a mommy, daddy, and two baby foxes out there behaving like foxes do to raise their family.

We watched our new neighbors for a week or so, but one morning they were gone never to be seen again.

Don't fall asleep. Look up. You never know what may be walking by. This is supposed to be a beach read, after all.

Two Jobs

When you get out of college and start your first job, your world changes. I know that many people work during the summer months to pay for college but it is not the same. Your mother and father develop an environment for you, and you are comfortable knowing and doing what you have to do. There are few uncertainties., but not many. All of a sudden, you are on your own. This could be the first time that you are alone. Just about everything that has to be done, you have to do it alone. I know that in college, you have decisions to make, but the social environment decides for you, through dormitories or fraternities or professors or something. What clothes to wear. What to eat. When to wake up in the morning. When to go to sleep. What to do if you are on a business trip. Should you order dessert after dinner? As I have said, your world changes.

Things happen in your business position, also. People operate in strange ways, and sometimes, it is really unusual. You wonder if you should follow their lead. Simple things like when to go to the bathroom and the coffee room are stupid examples. But maybe not. It is where you find out what is going on, and also make friends that may come in handy. They always say 'play it by ear'. But you can't play everything in the complex modern world by ear.

Here is what happened to a friend of mine. Actually, it is the next door neighbor. He worked in a large aerospace company. As is often the case in such organization, there is a thing called security, and there are two methods of maintaining that security. One is to make the total place secure, and the second is to have the employee to maintain his own security. Accordingly, it is sometimes the case that a manager does not even know what an employee that works for him or her is doing, and in what area of the building. When you would ask the manager what that employee is doing, he would say 'don't know".

In my neighbors group, there was a person from New York who came to work and deposited his outer coat and briefcase and left saying,"I'll be back." He never came back before my neighbor left in the evening for dinner. Apparently, they never found out. But I have an opinion. Later.

I worked in a company that had offices and cubes. I had an office and frequently passed a guy in one of the cubes that made his own coffee right in his cube. I talked to him pretty often as he was in the way to somewhere that I had to go. I asked him why he made his own coffee, and he said that he liked it better. He was a nice guy. It came that the management found out he was working two jobs. One in the morning until noon and the other from noon until 5:00 or so in the same area of the city. He got fired from both jobs.

He called me a couple of weeks later and told me he had started a company and already got a big contract. He wanted me to come and work for him for a quite big salary.

You can only guess if I took the job or not. Back to the first case. I subsequently felt that he had two jobs, but in the same company. I guess I'll never know.

Other Machines on Watch

I was working my way through college and was lucky enough to get a job on the assembly line at the foremost American car maker. It's your guess to determine which one it was. I made good money, as much as workers who had a wife and four kids. Of course, I was in the union. It was in my last year; one semester to go. I was a math major and the professor said pay attention, watch everything I write on the board, copy your notes right after class, and do your problem sets the very evening of your class – while it is fresh in your mind.

I must say, you get used to it, and it works. The classes were demanding but very interesting.

I worked a welding machine. I had to put an insert on an oil pan and weld them together. More specifically, I was on an assembly line. I had to take an oil pan off the line and put it on the welding machine. Then I had to place an insert for filling the oil pan on the oil pan, there were a big tray of them, and then push the buttons with both hand so I wouldn't get electrocuted. Bingo. It was welded. It's called spot welding. Then I had to put the oil pan that I just fixed up back on the assembly line and go to the next one. All evening long. The shift ran from 4 PM to midnight.

There were two of us and we both worked at full speed – the speed of the assembly line – for eight hours a day. It took about 30 seconds to learn your job, and the first few days were hard. If you didn't like it, that was too bad. If you complained that it was too hard, you were escorted out the door and they hired someone else.

Of course, everyone loved their job. And the funny thing was that after a few days, most of the workers actually did like their jobs. It is human nature.

In that environment, it was common to work on more than one machine for a variety of reasons, such as an employee didn't show up. That's then only reason I can remember. As an employee walks from one place to another, you would see an employees working on many different machines. If you are brain dead, you just put your head down and waddle by. If you have a brain that works, you see what that employee is doing and how he does it. I use only 'he' here, because only men worked on the assembly line.

It's like being in math class, and trying to remember everything you see on the board.

Well, I was a kid with a smile on his face and big biceps and was a math major. Then one day, I was asked — well not exactly ask — to work on a machine that involved handling quite large pieces of metal. The foreman can to me and said I will show you how to do it. Now this is the most important sentence in the whole speech. I said, "I know how to do it."

He was highly flabbergasted. He asked how I knew it, and I said I was just walking past the machine and saw the man working on it. I remembered it. Between you and me, I really liked walking around seeing how workers did things. I got recognition for my work.

I was asked to go to foreman training school. It had never been done before. Here is how I responded. "Thank you. I really like working here, but I have only one semester to go for my diploma and I think I should finish school."

It was a big decision for me. If I went to work, I would get drafted. If I went to graduate school, I would only avoid the draft until I graduated. But luckily, a large aerospace company came along and I would work on military projects and avoid the draft. I took the latter. I've lived a successful life, but have wondered how it would have been working in an industrial position, like I have just described.

Cans and More Cans

My dad was a good baseball player. In our city, there was sandlot baseball. It started with class F for young kids, E for organized baseball, class D and D backed, C backed, B backed, and A backed that was for major leaguers who just made it to the majors and needed the practice. When the great Bob Feller, the hall-of-fame pitcher, came from an Iowa farm to the Cleveland Indians, without going through the minor leagues, he pitched a few games in class A. Most people regarded class C was for high school ball, B was for college ball, and A was for the best. In my own case, I went up to class C.

"Backed means having someone play for the uniforms and get endorsement in return."

In those days, married couples and their kids visited other families. They talked about better times, if indeed they really existed, and usually had something to drink ranging from pop, coffee, and perhaps to alcoholic beverages that were rare in those days, following prohibition.

My dad had a friend name Vince Coleman that he played with. They were on the same team. Coleman was a big star and was offered a contract by a major league team. There was a catch. He would have to start in minor league AAA because he was young and inexperienced. AAA is as high as you can good go in the minors. In those days, the players chewed tobacco because of the dusty fields. Vince Coleman's father said major league or no. There were good jobs with the oil companies, such as Standard Oil. The team said no, so Mr. Coleman ended up in American business.

Now Vice Coleman was tall, rather muscular, and very friendly. He also chewed. In one visit to our home, Mr. Coleman asked me for a can. I knew it was for his tobacco chewing. Kids knew everything in those days. So I went into the kitchen and retrieved a large tomato can from the trash. My mother was beside herself; she had a new living room carpet. I put it on the floor next to Coleman. After a good chew, Coleman let fly and the spit landed directly in the can. So that was it for the day. Several spits, all right in the can.

A few weeks later, the Colemans visited again, and Mr. Coleman again asked for a can. What you don't know was that I was kind of a mischievous little kid ready to take a good chance. Again, I was asked for a can and I went into the kitchen as before. This time I selected a smaller soup can, and my mother was so mad at me that you couldn't believe it.

I brought the can into the living room and Mr. Coleman had a smile on his face. He was a wise guy and knew what I was up to. After another good bit of chewing, Mr. Coleman was ready for a spit. You could feel the tension in the room. Again with kind of a smile, he hit the can right in the middle. He had a bigger smile this time. Now you can guess the end of the story. Or, can you?

Another few weeks later, the Colemans visited again. My Dad and Mr. Coleman were good friends over many years. He was passive about this chewing, but this time my mother was on his case. It was also time for me to stop screwing around. This time Mr. Coleman, probably a demon in disguise, had a big chew and asked me again for a can. I do not remember after all of these years, what his expression was.

My mother had been on my case since the previous visit about the chewing, spitting, and the cans. I was getting a bit tired of being the object of her anger. So I decided to pay her back. I might have been a kind of devil, but I shouldn't say that. When I was asked for another can, I selected the smallest can I could find. Now she was mad and Mr. Coleman had a bigger smile that ever. He might have also been a devil in disguise.

Mr. Coleman took a big chew and let go with largest spit of all time. It landed right in the middle of the little can. Someone upstairs was looking after us. Mr. Coleman got transferred to California and the last I heard, he was the President of the company.

This is a real true story.

The Gym Class

Sometimes we live in difficult times and this read was one of them. We had a war going on and most of us thought we might get drafted right out of high school. Some of our physical education classes were devoted to military activity like boxing, rope climbing, marching, running 2 miles in cold weather with gym shorts on, and climbing those rope structures for climbing into things, like combat vehicles. This read is about that but it gets worse. In fact, most of us knew at least one person, a classmate that did not make it out alive. It was scary, so we took thing seriously.

I have a friend that seemed to be the object of unfair behavior, especially on the part of teachers, and in particular gym teachers. I had two situations. My friend was small in stature, maybe about 5 feet 1 inch or so weighing 95 pounds. Actually, I was also a little small, so I had sympathy for him. Whenever they needed an example, it was he.

Let's go back a few months. Now we are talking about my friend and not me. A boy in his neighborhood on the next street, got a boxing set for Christmas. It had two sets of head gear and two sets of boxing gloves. His father thought he should toughen up a bit. You know how boys in a neighborhood are, they know everything. It took a half day to spread the news of the Christmas present. The boy's mother backed her car out of the garage so the boys had somewhere to box. No one knew very much about boxing but most boys knew a things or two from their father or friend. Information spread rapidly, so in two days, they all were good boxers, and they practiced religiously. My friend was one of them.

Back to the story. There happened to be a boy in the high school named Ezzo. His father wanted him to be a boxer, for some unknown reason, and Ezzo started boxing in AAU matches. The faculty was interested and encouraged Ezzo regularly, who finally made it to the championship bout. Ezzo lost but he was the star of the school.

Back to the military training in gym class. It so happened on the day in question that the gym teacher was teaching about boxing and how to do it. Then, he said they would have Ezzo give a demonstration. My friend was selected as the opponent. Everyone thought that Ezzo would KO my friend, but they had a surprise in store for them.

They danced around and finally Ezzo threw a knockout right cross. My friend dodged it and returned with a left hook that knocked Ezzo on his keester. The teacher ended the boxing demonstration. But, that is not the end of the story.

The boys in my neighbor also went regularity went to the YMCA to do their exercises. Rope climbing was one of them. They were trying to get strong enough to climb the rope without using their legs, as they do in the circus. It was déjà vu all over again. The teacher was talking about it and mentioned how hard it was. He wanted to show that it was really hard to do. He thought that was true, but teachers don't know everything and sometimes don't know anything. Again my friend, who weighed 95 pounds, was told to try it. The dumb teacher made another mistake. Now the ceiling was high because it was an arena. My friend climbed about 20 feet with his arms alone and the teacher yelled "Stop, stop, you'll get hurt."

My friend climbed the rest of the way with the usual method and touched the ceiling. He the slid down the rope, and gave the teacher a big smile

My friend lived a successful life and grew in size and capability in spite of teachers not liking him. It was what he thought but never knew for sure or really didn't care.

But here is the rest of the story. At a neighbor get-together, my friend and his wife were talking with a couple they hadn't seen before. The couple spoke with a foreign accent. The man asked my friend where he lived in his city. My friend said, "The west side, it was annexed by the city." The other person blurted out, "That is where the Nazis live." My friend had a Jewish sounding name, given by US Immigration. My friend then knew his suspicions were true.

This a true story, down to the last letter. And now we know how things are.

Cheating in Class

It was a graduate course in Computer Science. There were students from many states and as many countries. They had come to the University because a professor had written a computer book and it gave the University an identity in the new field of computers. There were few undergraduate programs so the entrance requirements were straight forward: have a bachelor's degree in math, engineering, or a hard science with a good grade point average. Hard science was physics, chemistry, and similar programs. The first course was hard in order to bridge that gap between programs.

There was one student in the course from a small university in New Jersey named Fairleigh Dickinson. It had a popular name of Fairly Ridiculous. It was and is a good school that turns out scholars. In this case, he was the center of attention.

The foreign students had it tough. They had two problems. They had to be able to speak English and the travel, living, and tuition were expensive for students from most countries. The university about which this read was written had a liberal policy about bridging the international problem.

In an initial meeting with the department chairman, he had to ascertain whether the student knew enough English to be successful. If they did not know English, they had to take a course on it in their home country. That's the start of the problem. Their foreign teacher had to certify that the student was English competent, and in many cases would lie to protect their reputation. What was the department chairman to do. Here's the method. In the first meeting, he would remove his wrist watch and place it out of sight. Then he would say to the student, "I've forgotten my watch, can you tell me what time it is?" If the student answered "Yes", he would give the student another chance, "I've been in all day, is it raining outside?" If he got another yes, then the student was told he or she would have to take a free English course before taking the first class. The University never had a problem in that regard. The English instructor was the best that could be found.

Next problem was the course work. There was a lot of knowledge to be made up so the course was a killer. The professor was kind and gave a lot of extra attention to the students, foreign and American. Oh, I almost forgot. The entrance requirement was the same for Americans. The course had a special book written for it, and the first class received a manuscript copy lovingly printed at IBM, when they still sold copiers, The title of the book was and is *Advanced Programming: Programming and Operating Systems,* published in 1970. Now, it's time for the rest of the story.

During the first exam, the professor sat at the table in front of the class, paying little attention to the students taking the exam. There was about 50 student in the course and the last row was only partially filled. It was a new building and there was plenty of room.

The professor looked up and the student from Fairly Ridiculous – the scholar – was motioning with his head toward the rear. The happened 3 or 4 times, so the professor walked to the back row. Siting there was a foreign student next to an empty seat with his book wide open reading the answers. This was a case for a grade of F and probable expulsion.

But, what about the student? It could be that his parents had mortgaged there home to pay for his son to get an advance degree in a new subject – computers – in the United States. What did the professor and department do. He talked to the student and had him take another exam. The student graduated with his master's degree with high honors.

This is a true story, and I hope the student is reading this.

Harry Katzan Jr.

Shining Shoes

This is a doozie of a story. I was the oldest of a bunch of kids; actually it was only 4. But there were a number of years between #1 and #2. So, I got all the jobs, but I wasn't exactly collecting jobs, like mowing the lawn, shoveling the snow, and weeding the victory garden. Victory gardens were a part of the war, but the name kind of stuck.

When my father had a project, he always needed a helper that was generally a gofer. Gofer is a person that goes for things, like a saw or a hammer. Actually, being a helper is a good thing, because you learn about things that you ordinarily wouldn't even think about. I was the gofer. A good gofer.

My father was big deal in the church. He was the top dog in doing things for the church. He must have enjoyed it or was looking for a direct route to heaven. Every Sunday, he and another guy took the offering. They passed around a container into which the congregation put money to help keep the organization going, so to speak. It's called the offering plate.

By this time in my life, I had perfected the technique, that if you did a poor job, you wouldn't be asked to do I again. I had tried it on shoveling the snow and mowing the lawn, and I did not have great success, but I was in the process of perfecting my skills.

Every Saturday night I was expected to polish my father's shoes so he could look dapper out in the congregation with the collection plate. The process involved going to the closet and retrieving the shoes, shoe polish, and the brush with which to buff up the shoes on which I was expected to put the polish. Well, I must admit that I did do credible job with administering the polish and buffing the leather of the shoes. But somehow, I did not polish the area around the bottom of the shoe by the sole. Of course, that isn't the shoe, which was my argument. After a 15 minute discussion over the viability of polishing the sole around the shoe, I have to admit that I did it. But I was polishing my argument. Actually, I was good at it. Real good.

Finally, after several weeks of contest, my father was so angry at me that he said, "Are you stupid?" My response was perfect. "I guess I'm too stupid to polish your shoes."

My father must have thought that he was the King of England, because he would ask me to get his shoes and suit on Sunday morning before church. Actually, he didn't ask. We were always in a hurry with a father, mother, 3 kids, and an idiot getting ready for church. You could never imagine how many times my father went to church with a black shoe on his left foot and a brown shoe on his right foot. Achieving success with the shoes, I attempted the same with the trousers and suit coat, and I achieved great success.

Finally, my mom stepped into the game, and the fun was over. Believe it or not, what I just told you is true, down to the last syllable.

Football Kicker

Every kid wants to be on the football team. For some, it's to please their mother or father, and maybe someone else in the family or even someone outside of the family. For boys, it might a girl or the hope for a girl. Even girls would like the acclaim achieved through the game. They were cheer leaders. Who knows? No one really cares. But that phenomena exists.

A high school football team usually has 40 or so players, consisting of 3 teams – called the first string, second string, and the third string. There are also specialty players, like punters, extra point kickers, field goal kickers, and specialists on the special teams, such as the kickoff squad and the receiving team. Maybe the number 40 is too low, but it doesn't matter. What really matters, is that there are a lot of potential players that are vying for those spots. Perhaps two hundred or more in large high schools.

During tryouts, early in the season – perhaps late August – boys tried out for the school's football team. The tryout period lasted a couple of weeks and the coaches tried to choose the best persons for the respective spots on the team. Those that don't make it are lucky. Whoops! A slip up. They are quite sad. Because, making the team is a pretty big deal to high school players.

A quick remark. Of the 3 strings or teams of players, who plays the most football? The third stringers. Not in actual gamers, but in practicing. The first and second teams have to run plays against someone, and low and behold, it is the third string.

To continue, there is some monkey business going on. Not bad monkey business, but good monkey business. There are some kids that are a little small. Actually, they are little squirts. They mature later. Remember, we are dealing with high school kids and education, for lack of a better name, that is supposed to be the name of the game.

Some boys know the game through neighbor or other activity. They can do everything correctly, like blocking, tackling, running, and throwing, but they are just too small, So some coaches chose the little squirt to be the kicker, usually the extra point and field goal kicker. Consider it done.

One of the boys that did not make the team because he had a heart murmur or was a lousy player has a father who is a big time lawyer. The lawyer goes to the head coach and pleads the case for his son – probably with a handful of that green pursuant called money.

The result. The lawyer's son with the heart murmur is given the kicker slot. The little squirt that made the team is still on them team, but on the third string.

Now you know the rest of the story.

Big Money

I once worked at a U.S. Government research facility. Everything was top secret. You had to have a secret clearance to get hired. But once you got there, you couldn't go inside the facility until they obtained a special secret clearance for you. You could do your work, but just couldn't get inside. You had to work in special offices in the lobby. These were the days after the President John F. Kennedy assassination. I was coming from an aircraft facility in Texas and my special clearance was delayed because the FBI was busy with the events. My associate was coming from the aircraft facility in the North West. That facility is referred to as The Nehman Company. His name was Harold Burnside. Actually, those named are made up, but the events are true.

On Harold's first day inside the research facility, a long-time employee of the research facility met Harold and the first thing he said after he heard his name was, "Are you the Harold Burnside that modified our computer software and saved us several million dollars?" Harold replied, "I think it might be me, but I didn't know my work had been spread around, especially here with all of the security."

Here is Harold's story. He was a highly educated top-notch computer designer and programmer. When they had computer trouble, they called Harold even though it was the middle of the night. Harold worked on computer software that was used to manufacture missile components that could not be outsourced. He was valuable to the firm. After a couple of years, Harold asked to transfer to the systems group to make better use of his talents. He was still employed and in case of an emergency, he could be called upon. Harold was 25 years old. At 25, your brain is at top notch capability.

Harold's group had its usual weekly meeting and the manger mentioned that computer time was being used up and they would have to purchase a $7 million computer to meet the company's obligations to the government and meet its schedules. There would be a delay since many companies were having the same problem. When the Manager mentioned the problem, Harold said, "I can solve your problem." The Manager was totally surprised and the others in the room came out with remarks like, "He can't do it. He is as crazy as a bedbug." Harold had gone to 6-week computer school and knew the system like the back of his hand. The manager said go ahead and asked how long would it take. Harold said a week. Remember Harold was 25 years old and knew the computer system inside and out. He had paid close attention in the class after years of mathematical study.

In one week, Harold was done and the change worked like a charm; the company saved a lot of money. The Manager was overjoyed.

Here is what Harold did. He realized what was slowing down the computer was the input and output. Why not overlap it. Instead of waiting for input and output, buffer it. Put the input or output is a buffer and go to another application until the input or output was finished. Then go back to the original program. It's called buffering and permits the computer processing unit to work all of the time. Then the company distributed Harold's work to other companies via a Share organization. So all users of the computer could benefit from Harold's work. Of course, the computer company should have done this. Perhaps they did not do it in order to get more revenue.

Harold asked to go to a Share meeting, and an upper manager said, "He's just a kid. He would just sit there." Harold heard that and sent out his resumé.

This is a true story. It could have been described better, but that is a job for Harold.

The Broken Window

This is another episode of playing softball in the street. It must be that kids prefer streets to real baseball fields, because when things are getting darker in the evening, streets have street lights. Anyway, we were playing at the manhole cover 4 houses down the street. It seems as though kids liked it better down the street because no one called the cops.

I was the batter and hit a foul ball straight up, down through the trees, and BANG right through the plate glass window of a house, which later became my greatest success in life.

The ball hit the window with a horrific noise. The other players headed to the woods – only figuratively speaking – yelling, "George! Run." I did not. My good home training must have kicked in. Then owner rushed to the front of the house. He was mad. Real mad. It must have happened before, at least twice, and the culprits ran for the woods. You heard that before too. He came to the door.

There I was. All I said was, "I'm sorry Mr. Robinson, I broke your window. I will pay for it." His madness went away like a shot. "You are such a good boy," he said. "Thanks for telling me. What is your name and where do you live?"

"My name is George, and I live 3 doors down," I said.

"Go get your father." That, I did. I told him what I had done. He didn't say a word, just got up and walked three doors down the street. No emotion what so ever. It was like he was going to get the newspaper, or something like that."

When he got there, all the owner could say was what a good boy my father had, and all that. Finally, my father said, "How much do we owe you?"

The owner acted like had never thought of that, and finally said, "Twenty dollars."

My Dad pulled out his wallet and gave him a twenty, and said, "I'm very sorry about this."

The owner said. "Thank you, you have a very good son."

On the was home, my father was very happy and held my hand for the first time that I could remember. He said. "You owe me 20 bucks."

I don't believe I ever paid him back. My Father had turned into my Dad.

Army Anecdote

My lifetime buddy and pal Jimmy who lived down the street, and walked up to the corner to see what was going on, a million times – well not exactly that many. He had an older brother named Daniel. We all called him Danny. This is a very short story about him that I am calling an anecdote.

Danny was nice looking and was as sharp as a whip. He was a good athlete but never played anything. He didn't watch much, just stayed home. He was an expert hunter and loved that kind of activity. He was a crack shot with their 12 gauge shotgun and the 30-30 rifle. He was best at deer hunting, and could clean a deer in 30 minutes. Both of our families did not have much money so we spent a lot of our time talking and played those pocket knife games boys used to like playing in the soft grass around our homes. There was a war going on – it seems we always were in a war. At least that was what we thought growing up in that era.

We were worried because when we turned 18, we could get drafted. If you went to college, you were deferred until you finished college. You couldn't win. So we talked a lot about being a soldier and worked at getting into good shape. We could climb and run with the best of them. We were also strong. We all could bend a bottle cap with one hand. We could easily do 20 chin ups and 100 pushups with ease. We followed the war in the newspaper. Day by day.

Danny was the deep thinker. He was always trying to figure things out. For example, his family bought a record player and my family bought a piano. Who was better off? His mother finally answered the question for us. Every time I went to his house, his mother would ask me if I was still playing the pie-ana.

Danny surprised us and probably his mother and father, as well. When he turned 16, he dropped out of school, and sat around without a job, until he was 18 and he was drafted.

Apparently, he did well on the test they gave, and they offered to send him to Army school to finish his high school education. He declined. In gun shooting he strip and put back together his piece – what they called the M1 rifle and M1 carbine. For shooting, he failed terribly even when almost every other recruit got a sharp shooter award.

We never knew what he did in the Army but after 2 years, he was out. He got a very low paying job looking at water gauges for the water department. He retired with a city pension at age 65, and I had lost track of him.

Then, at a 'former neighborhood' social get together, he showed up. He was happy as a lark, with a beautiful wife, who had a lot of money. Now, I can't figure this one out. Can you?

Sports

This is a read about sports – well, not exactly. It happened after sports. The first incident happened in the dead of winter. We had snow, ice, wind, and other things I can't remember. It happened right in front of our house. There wasn't much traffic; actually there was no traffic. So we decided to have a hockey game with skates, hockey sticks, and a puck. There were about 10 of us. As they say, be prepared. We needed a slicker surface, so we ran a hose from my family's house to the street, and it did the job.

I have to admit that the playing skills of the 10 of us was not too great. A fall every once in a while was expected. We were kids. Then I got banged in the mouth by someone's elbow in a little hockey skirmish. It wasn't bad at all except my tongue was out. And we all saw red, like you know what. There was no one home in my house, because my mom was at the church. So, up to the church I went, and found my mom in the rec room amongst a big bunch of women.

My mom said, "Why are you here?"

I opened my mouth and the group of ladies saw a lot of blood and you can guess the response. Someone called a taxi and a doctor was our destination. After 2 stitches on the top and 1 on the bottom, I was released to an evening of peace and quiet. I thought. When my father came home, he was not happy or sympathetic. I had to put rock salt on the street. I learned my lesson.

+++

Harry Katzan Jr.

Kids will be kids and it seems as though they never learn. My next episode was even worse.

We could have played some touch football in the street, but that was not good enough, so we decided to play the real thing with helmets and shoulder pads. We carved a playing field in some undeveloped land nearby. Two telephone poles marked the goal lines and end zones and the sidelines were delineated with somebody's lawn mower.

During a game, I received a long pass. Instead of tackling me, some big joker just jumped on my back and I heard my right knee snap. That ended the game, and Danny, from the Army reads, rode me home on his handlebars.

The next morning, my father had to take the day off, and we went to the hospital. Same doctor, the tongue guy, looked at the x-ray and said I would be OK if I refrained from running for a long while. He put an ace bandage on my knee. I was sidelined.

By the way, I was the doctor's last patient. He was going back to medical school to become an eye doctor.

Believe it or not, all of this a really true.

The Paper Company

This is an interesting story about a paper company for which I worked as a summer job when I was a high school student. It was the summer before graduation. I was making only $1 per hour, but those were the good old days.

I was a good worker and liked to work. I felt that the dynamics of a work situation were challenging. I wrapped reams of paper, pushed trays of paper around, and just about anything other people did not want to do. Most of the workers were older men and one foreign worker. His name was Joe Samari and I did not know from whence he came. He was friendly and a good worker. He liked Coca Cola, and it cost only 5 cents per bottle from a vending machine.

The preceding school year I took chemistry in school and liked it. My parents had previously given me a chemistry set for Christmas and I had done each and every experiment. As most kids do when studying hydrochloric acid, I had put a penny in a class with some acid and was amazed how the acid had eaten the penny. We also put coins on train tracks and watched as a train ran over them. Some of the time, we actually found the coin afterwards.

In our house, as they used to say it, we didn't drink soda – we called it pop – at all. If we were thirsty, we drank milk. My parents did not drink pop or alcoholic beverages. They drank coffee with canned milk. When we had an extra dime, we went to the corner drug store – that's what we called it – and had a cherry phosphate and bag of Fritos. Cokes were not off limits but all my mother said that too many weren't good for you. Times were different then and most people were not that interested in drinking pop.

Joe Samari loved coke and the price was right for him. On a light day, he only drank 6 to 8 bottles. I said to him while we were working side by side wrapping reams of paper that too much Coke wasn't good for him. By the way, a ream is 500 sheets. That was before they changed it to 300. Joe said that wasn't true. Coke was not bad for a person.

So I made an experiment. I bought a bottle of Coke and put it is a glass. Then I put a good penny in it. Then I said to Joe, "When you come back from lunch, that penny will be eaten partially away." He said I was lying, and went to lunch.

I switched coins to a coin previously damaged with acid. When Joe came back from lunch, we looked at the coins and Joe was shocked. He stopped drinking Coca Cola, his only pleasure in life.

I wasn't just ashamed of myself, but I was mad at myself. I hated what I had done and still remember it.

So that was a good lesson for me. By the way, someone told Joe about the joke that wasn't a joke.

College Fun

I wouldn't say that college is fun. Math problem sets, English themes, and Psychology labs could spoil a good day. On the other hand, that is exactly what everyday life is. For me, Math problems were a pleasure, as would be a theme to an English major. I liked Math. Nevertheless, some events were in fact worthy of note.

Our dorm was close to a railroad track and the conductor would blow his horn - I don't know what you would call it – as he passed. My roommate had a recorder for recording professors. He recorded the train whistle and bell.

Then at inopportune times, he would go out in the hallway and play his recording. Idiotic students would run out in the hallway, etc.

Two of my fraternity brothers, who didn't have much money and joined the fraternity only because the room and board were cheap, would go to the drive-in theatre and back in the exit. You would think that it wouldn't work, but they were successful every time.

We had hell week that has a very bad reputation. Not in our frat house. It consisted of a 20 mile walk, and at 10 miles, some renegade members secretly brought sandwiches and drinks. They were only baloney sandwiches, but who cares after 10 miles. After the walk, they were given a pill to make us feel better. It was food coloring and the pledges found out when they went to the loo. Oops, I meant restroom.

We did one more thing on hell week. The dynamics were clever. They had to clean the toilet blindfolded. Beforehand, the members cleaned the toilet with detergent and then medicinal alcohol. It was as clean as could be. Then we would put a peeled banana in it. Then blindfolded, a pledge had to clean it. Almost everyone figured it out beforehand, but every once in a while, someone didn't. And that was it for hell week.

Girls had 9:00 curfew, so all you could do was go to one of the taverns and drink 3.2% beer and smoke cigarettes. That is if you smoked. Most girls had a nickname, like cig-ee-boo. That was enjoyable because it was so simple.

At fraternity parties, we served red punch, but told the girls that it was slow gin. They frequently acted out the part.

One more story. My good friend was a psych major who wanted to do counseling. One of the pledges – students who were joining the fraternity – was away from home for the first time without supervision and drank too much beer and was drunk every night and missed classes. We monitored the pledges and gave instruction on how to eat properly and get good grades. Otherwise, the fraternity would be in deep yogurt from the university. My fraternity friend was trying to help the pledge that drank too much and I knew all about it. He was sent home. That is, the pledge. Many years later, when we lived in a nice place like Sun City that very pledge lived there with his wife and told people he was in our fraternity. But I knew better but only talked about it to my wife.

Funny thing. The only thing that I really liked about college was the courses. Isn't that the way it should be?

The Torn Shirt

There are some events that bug you for life, even though they are reasonably minor at the time. Every day we had homeroom at the same time. We were still in high school. In home room you always sat next to the same person, for all of your early education. The jerk sitting next to me was one of those guys that couldn't sit still and was always pushing, pulling, grabbing, and so forth. Everyone knows at least one person like that.

It was my birthday, and my parents gave me a nice shirt. I put it on for school, and my mom said not to because it might get torn or something. I say, "Mom, nothing ever happens at school."

Well, it did. We were 5 minutes into homeroom and the person sitting next to me tore it. So I slugged him. Right in his left eye. Always go for the eye and not the nose, because it lasts for several days and you will get better results. You just hit the jerk around the eye, so you don't worry about it. The homeroom teacher asked what was going on, as if he didn't already know. Good teachers have that kind of vision in which you see everything without looking. The result was that we had to see the principal at 4:30 quitting time.

So there we were at 4:30 sitting in front of the Principals office. You always had to wait for a while, a subtle form of punishment. It was where the teachers clocked out. They did that in those days. I just sat there with that angelic look that I had perfected by then. I had blond hair, and all of my head, eyes, ears, nose and mouth were in the right places.

The teachers paid little attention, as it was high school, and there was always something going on. My French teacher walked by. She was a real busy body. Please note that I don't use bad language, except when driving. And that doesn't happen very often. Here is what she said, "Donald, that was the idiot's name, I'm so sorry." The she looked at me and said "George, I could have expected that of you." That's not my name but I had to use something.

Now that really irritated me since that teacher did not know what had happened.

The Principal was nice. Donald went in first and I do not know what transpired. When I went in, the Principal had a grin on his face and asked me what happened. I told him what had happened. He said we couldn't have fighting around there, and if it happened again, I couldn't be on the track team. And that was it. I was getting a good reputation, and that was meant to be a self-complement. In all of high school, I had perfect attendance and made the National Honor Society, and only slugged two boys. More in another read.

However, that French teacher was in my sights. I knew how to fix her. One of the things she didn't like was the same students putting their hands up when she asked a question. Now I really liked French class and I had 4 years of it. It could be the best language in the whole wide world.

Every time bag-o asked a question, I put up my hand, and I always sat in the first row. She was irritated more than I was. The girl behind me egged me on by tapping me on the shoulder and said raise your hand. After a couple of days, the whole class knew what was going on. They played along with me and didn't raise their own hands. This went on for a while and she finally figured out what was going on. She was a good teacher.

See you in another read.

The Bully Gets It

When I entered the high school age, it started I was a little squirt, and I was a target for all of those psychological nuts that roam the hallways and school yards looking for easy prey. Even when they were being friendly they bullied. They would use your head like a basketball. The hallways between classes were the only safe times. We had hall guards.

In our instance, a hall guard was a teacher, like an ex-NFL football player assign to monitor the hall ways on a rotational basis. Things were different in those days. Teachers could do anything. So if a hall guard caught a bully, that bully would wish he wasn't born for a few days. They started by grabbing you by the shirt and throwing you against the wall. You probably know the rest.

I was not having any trouble in my classes. I excelled in math and science but the English class was a problem. I loved to write and excelled at it. Normal reading was duck soup, except for the stuff the teacher liked. So I had to adopt the writer's defensive position. Read the first chapter and the last chapter and hope for the best. My parents asked me about school and I knew it was about bullying. My parents were educated and knew full well about bullying and related behavior. I said I was getting a lot of bullying and my father mentioned the German method. Get your friends and beat the tar out of the person doing the bullying. My mother had a fit. "Don't go around talking about the Germans in wartime." So, I felt that another method was in order. For me, it was just a few seconds and I had a plan.

In gym class, we played basketball a lot and the two teachers stood by the sidelines and watched. One guy, about 12 inches taller than I, was really giving me the business, knocking me all over the place. I think the teachers were waiting to see how I would solve the problem. They probably thought that I would complain to the teacher like a little baby.

I'll tell you, that's not me. So my plan was that after a particularly tough run down the court, slug the guy. It would be a fight and the other kids would break it up. So on D-day, I did it. We ran down the court and he was hitting shoving me all the way. When we got under the basket and he was not prepared, I slugged him in his left eye. Not the eyeball, but the whole eye socket. He would have the biggest black eye that money could buy. The teachers never said a single word and the bullying stopped for good.

Let's say the bully's name was Bob Bully, and my name was Al Smart. The kids, and girls as well, would say "What happened to Bob Bully," The answer was always, "He bullied Al Smart, who slugged him."

I was the hero. It's a true story.

On an English Road

It was during World War II that an American officer and his driver, a Sergeant, were in England traveling between air bases to check out modified aircraft. Along one long stretch of muddy road, they came upon a young woman who had slipped off the road while driving a light military truck. The officer stopped to offer assistance. It turned out that she was a Second Subattern (i.e., a second lieutenant) in the women's Auxiliary Territorial Service. Her specialty was mechanics and truck driving. Assisting with the war effort was an honorable thing to do for women at that time in history.

"Are you okay?" asked the officer.

"I'm okay," she answered. "I'm just a bit frightened. I've been off the road for a long while and thought that no one come by up to assist me. You are Americans?"

"We are both Americans," answered the officer. "Let us help you."

The jeep, a remarkable little vehicle, pulled her out of the mud, and the conversation continued.

"We are traveling to the RAF Grangemouth air base," continued the officer. "We work on airplanes."

"You are a Colonel. Do you fly airplanes?" The pretty young woman asked. "My name is Mary Wales, by the way."

"I am a pilot," answered the officer. Would you like some chocolate, or cigarettes, or nylons? We have chocolate and cigarettes from our K rations, and they give us nylons to give to women that we encounter. We know that some items are not available in England."

"I would appreciate some chocolate and nylons. I'm very hungry and have been waiting here for a long time."

"You are very brave," said the officer. "Most women don't want to help out with the war effort. You look like my sister. She is very beautiful."

"Thanks for the complement," replied Mary. "Can I give you a good old British hug?"

The officer replied, "Sure, and I'll give you an American hug in return."

After the hugs, Mary replied, "That is the first hug I have ever been given. People don't touch me."

"Nice looking girl," said the Officer. "I hope she makes it wherever she's going."

"You bet," said the Sergeant.

The Queen

A former American military officer and his associates were summoned to help solve a serious financial problem for the Queen of England. (It just happened to be the same American officer mentioned in Read #36`.) He subsequently was promoted to be General officer.

An associate related the following scenario. "The General and I were summoned to London to solve a financial situation in the Royal Monarchy. Sharply at 9:00 am, we were ushered into the Queen's office suite. She was dressed in a bright green dress with suitable jewelry. We were dressed in black suits, white shirts, and black ties. We offered a bow, and the Queen waved it off with a request that we be seated. The Queen was very sophisticated and comfortable with her position as leader of the Monarchy."

General Les Miller looked at the Queen, the Queen looked at the General, and both remarked at exactly the same time, "Do I know you?" The Queen and the General gave each other a big American hug, and the Queen said to the General, "I can still taste that chocolate bar that you gave me on that forlorn road during the war. I was so hungry. I saved the nylons that you gave me and still have them." The General replied, "When I saw you on that lonely road, I thought you were the prettiest girl I had ever seen. I still do."

I looked at the two of them in awe. Here was a Queen and a General behaving like a couple of college students. He would eventually find out, informally, that she also had a PhD that hardly anyone knew about.

Harry Katzan Jr.

The Queen also mentioned a downside of being Royalty. By the royal decree, no one is supposed to touch the King or Queen. For her, no person had touched her since her encounter with the American officer on that muddy road during the war. The General said that was indeed an unfortunate circumstance but guaranteed that he would not abstain from an occasional American hug – but not in public. Subsequently, the financial problem was solved and the Queen made one more request, "Would you take me on a date tomorrow? I know this is common among Americans, but not for Royalty."

The General responded he would enjoy doing that and agreed to make a plan for the day. Bright and early the next morning – and it was a beautiful sunny day – the Queen and the General set off on their date. They both dressed in plain clothes so as not to be recognized and were driven by a chauffeur in a plain English vehicle. The first stop was Harrods, where they looked at goods on each and every floor. The Queen remarked several times, "I can hardly believe that this is how people really shop and live. It is wonderful."

The General bought the Queen a beautiful black ball pen with the name 'Harrods' printed in gold on the side. The Queen looked at the General with a twinkle in her eyes and said they were not allowed to accept gifts from English people, but the rule said nothing about Americans. The couple spent hours at Harrods, and no one recognized them.

The next stop was the bar at the Ritz hotel. An end booth was reserved so that they could gaze out at the other patrons. The Queen had an American martini, and the General had a single malt scotch. They both lingered over their drink and talked about the differences between royalty and the normal citizen. The last stop was Simpson's on the Strand, where they each had a special roast beef dinner with treacle pudding for dessert. They were both very quiet on the ride back to the palace.

The Queen said, "This was the best day of my life. Thank you." She gave the General a sophisticated kiss. "It is quite amazing that I could go for one whole day and be recognized by no one."

The day with the Queen was over."

The First Lady

The President returned from a trip from the west coast, and as the hour was late, slept in the second bedroom of the White House. He had a policy of being at home every night, except for international travel. He went to the spare bedroom this night since the First Lady had a bad case of the flu and he did not want to disturb her. The President arose early the next morning, as was normally the case, to read the President Daily Brief. He was interrupted by an aide with the news that the First Lady was missing. The Secret Service had been alerted and all agencies of the government had also been alerted. The President said he did not want the public to be informed and all points of exit be alerted. After 24 hours, the director of Intelligence was summoned who contacted that his favorite problem solvers be summoned. They were rushed to the White House by a new electric supersonic aircraft. The problem solvers were known a Matt and the General.

Mr. George Benson, the President's go-to person was summoned, and he described the extent of the investigation of the problem to Matt and the General. "We can solve your problem," said Matt. "We will use methods that we have used before."

"We will use it on your problem," said Matt. "Here is how we should approach the problem of the First Lady. Your team from the FBI, CIA, and so forth, as good as they are, are going after the First Lady by looking in places she could be. They should be looking where she shouldn't or wouldn't be. So the question is, what are the places where she shouldn't be, and I guarantee there will not be too many of them around. So I would like a tour, together with the General, of the total scene of the investigation."

So they started on a tour of the entire scene, They ended up at the bunker in the Treasury Building and the tunnel leading there from the White House. The tunnel was constructed during World War II and was totally deserted. Along the way were many closed and locked rooms labeled 'Cot Room # xx, for use by support people in the event of an attack. The rooms probably hadn't been opened since they were constructed and were stocked with bottled water and k-rations in the 1940s. There were no keys to the rooms, since they never had been used. Matt said to Benson,"You should get the Army Corps of Engineers in here and open the doors."

It is amazing how quickly the Army Corps of Engineers can respond. In an hour, the first door was opened. Nothing. So they asked Matt what to do, and he responded as if they were a bunch of children, "Look at the handles. They are covered with 50 years of dust and dirt."

The engineers did as ordered and discovered one with no dust or dirt. They opened that door, and voila! There was the First Lady and the Secret Service agent.

Matt said, "Give me a few minutes with them." He was as cool as a cucumber.

If you have never seen Dr. Matt Miller, you should know that he is tall, slender, deeply tanned from golfing, and he speaks with a calm reassuring tone that makes a person respect him.

"We've been looking for you," said Matt. "A few people were getting worried. How did you get in here?"

"I had a key from World War II in the 1940s," replied the Secret Service agent. "Several of us were stationed here. I know I don't look that old, but I am."

"Next,. Ma'am, why are you here?" asked Matt. "I won't tell anyone. It's only between you and me. But, don't worry. I'll fix things up for you."

"I just have this awful flu and look at me," said the First Lady. "I look like a witch. I'm blubbering all over the place. I've been crying, and my hair is a total mess."

Matt said to the Secret Service agent, "Why did you do it?" "Because she asked me to. That's my job," was the answer. "I have to do what she asks or tells me to do."

Matt came out of the cot room, and asked Benson to call the President. "Tell him that the First Lady has been found and to come immediately to cot room #37 with her raincoat and a rain hat."

The President arrived in less than 10 minutes, and Matt said, "Be kind to her, Mr. President, she needs you now."

Matt and the General met with the President in his private office. "Thank you, gentlemen," said the President. "You've solved my crisis, and I will be eternally grateful. Please send me a bill for whatever amount you please."

"There is no need Mr. President," the General said. "Our work is gratis."

This read is a bit longer, but definitely worth it.

The Royal Baby

This read centers around Matt an established mathematician and a college friend named Ashley that aspired to be actress. While Matt studied his mathematics, Ashley worked in the entertainment industry. While Matt earned his PhD, Ashley made it as a TV star and attracted a Prince in the English Royal Monarchy. They were married in the English royal manner.

From day one, the English media and the paparazzi were against her for two reasons: she wasn't English and she was bi-racial, or rather, she thought so, and they thought she was bi-racial also. They were married in a glorious ceremony, but from the first day of their marriage, she was treated with disrespect. She had no privacy and had no control of her life. The Queen gave them a luxurious home to live in and she had all the money to live like a future Queen. Royalty must have children and before long she was childbearing, and the paparazzi went to work on her with full speed. At least the paparazzi and the media thought she was childbearing.

The princess called Matt in the United States; she did not want to be a mother and Matt and his wealthy friend went to work. They used their knowledge of the government scene and attracted a surrogate mother for the princess. Meanwhile, the paparazzi and the media centered around the size of her stomach and noticed it grew and noted that it must be a pad. As the size of her stomach grew, they wrote that she just increased the size of the pad.

The mother of the surrogate baby was approached concerning a possible role as a U.S. spy in England, which she turned down, However, she agreed to take on the role as a nanny of the surrogate baby. Her name was Emma Williams.

At just about the time that the royal baby was to have her baby, the surrogate mother gave birth in the states and the surrogate baby was transported to London in a secret airplane and transported to Ashley, the Prince's wife. The baby was born and no one knew if the baby was a real baby or a surrogate baby. The paparazzi and the media went wild and made Ashlley's's life miserable. However, the mother of the surrogate baby served as the nanny to her very own baby. She loved the position. For her, it was a good deal. The queen was a tricky old person and got the information about the spy business out of the nanny, even though that option was never exercised.

On a Saturday on her day off, the nanny looked the wrong way as she was crossing Charing Cross Road in London and was killed. To this day, the English people do not know if the baby is a real baby of Ashley or a surrogate.

Meanwhile back in the states, Matt and an academic friend determined that Ashley was completely Caucasian and not bi-racial. Her biracial parents were biracial and told Ashley that she was bi-racial to keep things simple.

One Last Thing

This is a read about how someone could spread a virus and get a Nobel Prize. It's not true and never will be. But it gives some food for thought.

A team of three experience biologists were investigating the origin of the COVID virus. They covered the subject quite well and even uncovered a mole in another country. Not to cast ridiculous thoughts, assume the county is named Lem. The trio covered the epidemic quite well and encountered a biology mole – that is a person who lives in Lem and feeds information back to the states. The team obtained knowledge of a well-known scientist in Lem that wanted to earn a noble prize. He came up with an ingenious plan. If a person invented a cure for the virus, he or she would for sure get that prize. The scientist was very well regarded in Lem and the entire world for knowledge and research on various problems in the area of biology related to infectious diseases. He determined that he could create in his lab a serum to give a person the COVID disease. He knew, based on his research, how to create an antidote to cure the disease.

Here was his plan. His country like all the rest, has training programs that prepare potential spies with needed information about a country, its customs and speech habits, and local ways of saying things. Each of the potential spies was sent to the country as a student, for practice in their spying capability. The scientist had his own research facility and could enable this plan. It was his plan and only his plan. He would infect a student of his through his or her favorite drink, like coca cola. He would send them to the various countries and infect the people. Of course, the virus would spread rapidly. They would go all over the free and non-free world. He could only get the Nobel Prize if people all over the world were infected.

His students would go into the world and infect many people. Through propagation of the disease, it would spread quickly. The students would come back to Lem and he would give them the antidote. So they would be free of the disease. However, in the process, he infected himself and died before he could finalize the antidote. None of the leadership of Lem and its President knew about this insidious plan. And that could be the origin of the virus we experienced.

LONGER STORIES

This is a group of stories that are a
Longer in length
And perhaps a little more
Complicated and more interesting

Where did That Computer Go

A few year ago, I was fortunate to be working for a computer company located in lower New York State. I had designed software for dual processor systems. That is, two computer processors running off the same memory but running separately. You have heard the saying, 'Double the workers, double the fun, work together to get more done.' Well, you probably haven't heard it because I just made it up. Perhaps it should read, 'Double the workers, double the fun, have two workers and get less done.'

I worked on error recovery, so the system would continue running, regardless of an underlying problem. I know the age old custom; just pull the plug and start over. Or, even worst, reload the operating system. Sometimes, you have to do that, as with ransomware.

Remember, there are two or more processors running at the same time. The throughout must be fantastic. An error is detected in one of the processors, and the hardware stops the processing in that processor. Then other processor stops, and sends a feeler to the stopped processor to check it out – just as a human would do. Actually, a human probably couldn't do anything, except call someone else.

The fun begins now. If the error in one of the processors occurs and that processor is in the supervisor state, then the whole system is brought down and a technician has to take a look at it, which amount to calling a systems programmer. If the error occurred in the problem state, then it is very complicated. If it a memory error, then the job is flushed and that chunk of storage is taken out of business and everything continues, and so on. That is not what his read is about.

With large computers, in both size and capacity, that total system is hand made. It has a platform in a large warehouse, and techs brings parts to it. The platform is labeled as the company that bought it. If it is government, it just says U.S. Government. It could be scheduled to go almost anywhere; Army, Navy, CIA, State Department, anywhere.

I had gone up for business and passed it on my way to where I was going on more than a few occasions. One particular day, it was gone. No one knew when or where it left. Even the hardware people did not know where it is.

And, that is the story, and the way it is.

From Outer Space

It all started for me anyway when the CIA released its library of information on UFOs. It perked my interest in what was actually going on in that area of technology. Now here is a question. Let's say I purchase a recreational drone and attach a flashlight to it. Do I have a UFO drone? Most of you would say absolutely NO. Then what is a UFO? I will look into that first, and then carry on.

At first I thought that the lights were part of the propulsion system that keeps the UFO up. There were 2780 CIA reports on the subject so it was hard to go through all of that stuff, and also, some of the reports had some sentences blacked out for security reasons. There was a series of events that opened the door on this subject.

A university wanted to open a research lab for Astrophysics. The scientists were American but the director was a person named Michael Davis, usually known as Prince Michael of the English monarchy, who has a PhD from Oxford and is quite an intelligent fellow. He was not treated nicely in addition to a temperament that did not blend well with American workers. He was not used to handling equipment and did not work long hours like most Americans. On one occasion he used the wrong equipment on the right thing or vice versa. He got interesting information, which I will cover later, and the Americans must have said the wrong thing to him So one day he just left and went back to England without telling anyone. There was something going on upstairs with him – that is, his brain – and we decided to look into it. Here is a brief summary of it.

> "It started out as a simple equipment error. I was going to use an astrophysics electron camera and focused it at a close distance rather than a far distance. It was a common error, as I was not accustomed to using the equipment. I viewed a large squadron of space vehicles headed for Earth. There was a very high number of them, and they appeared to be in complete synchronicity, probably driven by one computer or by individual computers operating in exactly the same way. The formation was without any deviation. Some of them were lighted as UFOs normally are. I focused the electron camera outward and observed that the squadron was emanating from within another galaxy. It appeared to be from the Pinwheel Galaxy that has a planet Zenex with identical characteristics to Earth. The lighted UFOs appeared to be leaders, and the others could be controlled by artificial entities."

Here is how my thinking progressed. The Defense Department had a project to develop a Closed Ecological System (CES). It was a cold war method for survival. In a CES, humans could live for an extended period in an enclosure containing water, plants, and a crop of fish. The humans could eat the fish. The planets could absorb the carbon monoxide, and so forth. The system was actually built and tested. People could survive for an extended period of time.

The UFOs with lights could be surveying the planet Earth and return to the Pinwheel Galaxy in a CES. It's pretty far back, about 21 million light years. A light year is the distance that light can travel in a year. But, time slows down at very high speeds so it is possible.

Then Zenex space ships, piloted by artificial intelligence and using nuclear power could be distributing phenomena, such as the COVID virus, to the entire world. When we are all killed, the inhabitants of their planet in the Pinwheel Galaxy, which is going extinct, could be transferred to Earth through a large number of CESs in space ships powered by nuclear engines and controlled by artificial intelligence.

There could be two types of UFOs: a lighted one that would transport human occupants, and a dark one that transports viruses and is driven by computers, and destroys itself over the ocean.

This is not a true story.

The Rescue

The Queen's son Prince Michael and his son, the Prince of Bordeaux, with the regal name Prince Philip George William Charles were missing. Prince Michael was an internationally known scientist with a PhD in astrophysics from Oxford, and was instrumental in developing a vaccine for the COVID pandemic. The reason for the kidnapping was not known and also where he was being held. Using diplomatic channels, the United States believed it was Iran. The major concern was that Iran was developing a nuclear weapon and they needed assistance on their project. The objective was to extract the Prince and his son out of Iran to a friendly country.

Then Intelligence developed a plan to use an Iranian spy turned to favor the Americans to locate the Prince and his son and use American personnel to perform the extraction. The Iranian spy, named Atalus, or Adam Benfield in the American domain, was selected to locate the son and the Prince and assist an American team that would perform the extraction. The team of Dr. Matt Miller, Ashley Miller, and Dr. Les Miller, known as the General, were selected to perform the complicated task.

The plan was to have the team go to Iran, locate the Prince and the son, and have Adam Benfield drive them at an opportune time to a deserted airfield to be picked up and transported to a neighboring country. Details of the operation were the responsibility of Matt, Ashley, and the General. The two main elements of their plan was to get the team into Iran and how to get themselves and the abducted victims safely out.

The exit vehicle was designed by Matt and the General as a modified drone to carry passengers, since drones were not considered to be a threat by the Iranians. Matt, Ashley, and the General were to attend governmental foreign language school to learn Farsi. The courses consisted of two-week total immersion followed by a one week of the methodology of covert operations and social interactions.

The drones were modified to take land and off from a grassy plain. The Iranian Sukhoi air field was deserted and could be used. Iran had ordered a fleet of Sukhoi fighter planes from Russia, and Iran built a special field for them. Then Iran experienced a budget problem, because the U.S. blocked their bank funds and the order was cancelled. The field – the runways and buildings – are unused and totally accessible.

Russian passports for Ashley, her male escort, Matt, and the General were obtained through the English Monarchy. Ashley and her escort would enter Iran through convential airlines since Ashley would be dressed like an Iranian woman. Meanwhile, Matt and the General would fly to the Drone Base in Israel. The drones will have been transported to the Drone Base in C-17 transport planes.

On the day of the operation, Ashley will fly to Tehran by an accomplish of Benfield's and Matt and the General will be transported to the Sukhoi air field by the drone. Benfield will pick them up and go to an expensive hotel. Ashley will become acquainted with little Prince Philip.

As an interesting sidelight, the General was more calm about the Iranian mission than he would normally be the case. Matt asked why, and the General was more that pleased to tell him that he had met two Iranian students when he was getting his MS degree in computer science in New York. The Iranians loved American life, especially beer, hamburgers, and American women. The President of the university was a financial consultant to the Shah of Iran and the two students were part of the deal. The two men were excellent students and one of them was even translating the professor's computer book to Farsi.

On the day of the penetration of Iran by the drone, the U.S. military planned for the mission and had an F-117 fighter based on an aircraft carrier as an escort. The American fighter plane was invisible to radar. Nothing occurred and the F-117 returned to the ship without incident.

The operation was planned on a religious weekend in Iran. Matt and the General were escorted by Benfield in a Mercedes S500 sedan to the meeting room. Prince Michael entered with two body guards and started to lecture in English. The audience seemed to understand English. The Prince's lecture on viral science was well prepared and very technical; it was not clear that the audience understood what was going on. Matt made eye-contact with Prince Michael, who recognized Matt and flicked his eye. Prince Michael and Matt knew each other. The reason for the abduction was virology and not atomic secrets.

The next morning, Benfield repeated his trip to the Biology building with Matt and the General. After about an hour, Matt and the General were approached by a tall Iranian officer. "Excuse me, do I know you?" he said to the General. "Did we attend the university together?"

The General looked at the officer and said, "Yes you do. We were in the same master's class together. You were from Iran, and your name is...". The General thought for a few seconds and said, "you are Robert Peterson, and your associate student was John Evans, and you were both from Iran."

"That's true," said Robert Peterson. "You have a good memory. My Iran name is different. I am the country's technology officer, equivalent to an American Vice President. I would like to talk to you."

Our cover has been blown, thought Matt. We are in big trouble. I'm going to have to figure out a way to get us out of this situation. The four men were escorted by a guard to a separate room.

The Iranian technology officer initiated the conversation. "My American studies enabled me to attain my high position. I can have you put in prison or even executed." The General swallowed and cleared his throat. Matt looked into his eyes and he saw fear.

"We are here to extract Prince Michael," said Matt.

"Why didn't you ask him to be a consultant to your country?" asked Matt.

"That is not the way things are done in Iran," said Peterson. "I have no control over that."

"I have a PhD in mathematics from a university in California," continued Peterson. "I know of you. You are a mathematics scholar. You are Matt Miller." Matt thought to himself that a bond had been made between the two men. His brain was working in high gear.

"Why did you do this?" asked the General.

"Our country is dying from then COVID virus, as you call it, and no country will provide us with a vaccine. We can pay for it," said Peterson. The General was totally flustered. Matt was as cool as a cucumber. "Can we make a deal?" asked Matt.

"All options are open," answered Peterson.

"Can you exchange the four of us – the General, your friend Atalus, Prince Michael, and me for a working vaccine for all of your country," asked Matt.

"I can do anything," said Peterson. "I have the power to release you as soon as you guarantee the vaccine."

I can give you an answer in minutes," replied Matt. "If you will direct me to a an outdoors area where I can make a satellite call to the U.S."

Matt called Kimberly Scott, a government associate in Washington on his wrist satellite phone. Kimberly understood the plan is seconds.

"We have plenty of vaccine" she said. "Let me call President Strong."

Kimberly responded in 5 minutes. "He will guarantee the vaccine free of charge to Iran if England will guarantee a minimal amount. Here are the figures. Iran has 80 million people. 60 million are adults. We will guarantee 40 million doses if England will guarantee 20 million. As a side comment, he will guarantee all 60 million, if necessary. He said England should give a little. After all, the guy Michael is from England. I have to call the General's old buddy Sir Bunday and he can contact the prime minister. Just give me a few minutes. Hold on."

"I have a response already," Kimberly said. "England will guarantee 20 million doses. The following is important to complete the transaction. We expect to transfer the vaccine in refrigerated trucks loaded into C-17s. We can load our 40 million doses into two refrigerated trucks in one C-17, and England can load their 20 million doses into one C-17, along with a truck. The three trucks in two C-17s will be delivered to Iran at Sukhoi air field in one week – probably 5 days. Iran has to guarantee they will do diligence and provide sufficient medical staff to handle the doses pf vaccine. We will provide two doctors and one nurse to train them. Who is your contact in Iran?

"Dr. Robert Peterson," said Matt. "He is VP of technology for the entire country and educated in the states." "Okay," said Kimberly. "We have him in our database. By the way, this Sir Charles Bunday, known as Buzz, is a wonder. I asked him how much he is getting for his work. He said $3 million and I raised it to $4 million."

"You are a nice person and a genius," said Matt. "I know," said Kimberly, "just doing my job. I hope to meet you some day.

Matt relayed the news to Robert Peterson, the General, and Benfield. Peterson was pleased beyond belief.

At noon of the first day of the holy season, Ashley and little Prince Philip were transported in an armor plated Mercedes S500 to Sukhoi air field. At approximately the same time, Prince Michael, the General, Matt, and Benfield were being transported in a similar car to Sukhoi air field.

The drone arrived at the scheduled time and the group was flown to the Drone Base in Israel. Everyone was transferred to London in the General's Gulfstream 650 and disbursed from there.

The Iranian Students

What would it be like to have two special foreign students, from a country that was not particularly friendly. The President of the University was a consultant, in better times, with the Shah of Iran. The two students were part of the package. They had good backgrounds in electrical engineering and were graduate student in computer science.

The student did well and liked the freedom we have in America. The really liked hamburgers, beer, and the friendliness of American men and women.

They completed their Master of Science in Computer Science in two years, as excellent students. There were only three incidents.

The computer science program had a large budget than the chairman had to sign off on each month. It amounted to travel, conferences, supplied, equipment rental, office supplies – since the math and physics departments had no budgets and used the computer science department for assistance. The computer science department also had a budget for copy machine charges and the telephones. The telephone had a fool prove lock that no one had ever penetrated. For one month, there was an enormous charge for a call to Iran,. Ever one denied any wrongdoing. So what was the chairman to do. So what was the chairman to do? The answer was the easiest of the world. Nothing. Sign the form and hope no one in administration noticed it. It worked, but someone learned his lesson.

One of the Iranians was translating the professor's textbook into

Farsi. When asked why, he had not answer. The answer was simple. There are many crimes in the modern world of the stealing of IBM computers. But you can't steal IBM manuals and textbooks in their languages.

That same student was in big trouble for another thing that was more serious, That student really like the departmental secretary. She was Hispanic, her skin was Iranian color,; she was nice looking with a good figure, and he was hooked.

He asked her for a date 3 times and she denied him. She had a boyfriend and she did not particularly like him. Finally, he offered money and the situation went to the departmental chairman, who had a long talk with him about American customs and acceptable behavior. He had never had anyone talk to him in that manner, and he learned fast.

To put it bluntly, it's all in a day's work, as they say.

To France and Back

Countries differ on how they tax their citizens in order to run their country. Most, these days, tax on income. France charges on income and how much money you have in the bank. So many, if not all, citizens put their money in a Swiss bank. For years, the country of France has been trying to find out who these people are.

On a particular occasion, a Swiss bank in Geneva needed to have a tape taken from Geneva in Switzerland to a branch bank in Lausanne Switzerland. An employee was going between branches by car and another employee asked him to take a tape to Lausanne. Because of the geography, the fastest way was through France. On his way, the employee could stop in a bistro for a glass of wine and talk to the girls.

On the way back into Switzerland from France, the employee was stopped at the border. "Anything to declare?" asked the French border person. "No," said the driver. "What's on the back seat?" France had the tape they had long tried to get.

France had the tape with hopes of finding French citizens names, and so forth. They tried to read the tape but couldn't because the French banks use IBM computers and the Swiss bank uses Unisys, previously known as Sperry Univac.

They approached a Swiss bank employee with a lot of money to get a program enabling them to read the tape. He gave them a program, but at the last minute he, was loyal to Switzerland, gave them a program but not the right one. France got mad and turned him in to the Swiss bank management.

Both employees were tried in a court and sentenced to many years in prison for violating Swiss banking laws.

The Swiss bank tried to use software encryption to protect their data, but it took too long to do the calculations, so they had to resort to hardware encryption.

This is not a long read in words, but in importance, it is a long read. You should read it twice.

What Happened to My Data

When a dishonest person gets into your computer and takes over the software and locks the data files using cryptography and you have to pay to have them unlocked, it is called *ransomware*. Actually, the name reflects the name of what the program that does the dirty work is called. There is no name for the creeps that do it. If a person that does ransomware is caught, they should be given life in prison, because this is serious business. Innocent people's lives are at stake.

Sometimes, the files are important, like in a hospital, but not all of the time. Students that had their files locked asked what to do and were told to just reload the system software. But, when it involves infrastructure computers, like with oil companies, electric suppliers, and hospitals, the situation gets serious and the company just pays the requested money. It has already been as high as a million dollars. Sometimes the criminals lock the entire computer. It seems there is a conceptual model behind the criminal use of ransomware and it is something like the following. A computer operator get bored in the middle of the night just sitting there and handling computer operations. He searches on the Internet until he gets an interesting link and then he clicks on it. The malware, as it is called, is loaded and takes over the computer.

Here is how it works. Some event happens and the malware is loaded onto the computer to be invaded. It is well written software usually called smart software. It starts looking around until it finds something interesting. It uses its cryptographic software to lock the data file or database. It threatens that it will destroy the data and requests money to unlock it. Customers could be large or small, but large customers are a good target.

This is a terrible problem because users like a hospital are involved the people's lives are at stake. The users usually have to pay using bitcoin and the U.S. government is on their tail. Some of the bad guys are in Russia because the government has no law against doing it. However, the Russian government is not involved with it and is also known to be the victim.

Major software companies are addressing the problem.

Please Be Careful

It happened to a close friend of mine; actually a college roommate. His name is Walter Baldwin. We studied our math together, and through his wit and temperament, we both did well. He has a good and beautiful wife, an outstanding son, and an also beautiful daughter, named Kimberly Baldwin. This is really her story.

Kimberly met Sam Peterson in a freshman psychology course. He asked her if she would like a cup of coffee with him at the local Starbucks, and she said yes. He was a nice boy, not particularly handsome by American standards, but active and friendly. He was on the soccer team and could run like the wind. Most of all, he was very attentive to Kimberly; he was a good catch. Kimberly was a nursing student and Sam liked that; he frequently asked her about her nursing studies. Kimberly desired a career in emergency nursing, and the money was good. It was a tough job and the hours would be long. Sam didn't seem to mind.

Kimberly and Sam dated together for four years and they graduated at the same time. Kimberly chose a hospital in Chicago and by chance Sam got an engineering job in the same city. Things went well but an engagement never came.

One Christmas, Sam's mother visited Kimberly and told her that Sam would be going to visit his brother in Iran to work on an engineering problem that was in trouble. At first, Kimberly was totally shocked. She loved Sam and she thought he loved her. What was happening? Why hadn't Sam told her personally.

Finally, Sam's mother told Kimberly that they were Iranian and had adopted the common English name of Peterson. Kimberly was devastated but soon got over it. Sam was just afraid to tell Kimberly that he was Iranian; he loved her so much and was afraid that she would reject him. Kimberly told Sam's mother that she still loved Sam and that everything would be okay when Sam returned to the U.S.

Then, out of the blue, Sam's mother called Kimberly and said that Sam was deathly ill and needed her attention. Kimberly really loved Sam; he was so kind and gentle and always good with financial affairs. She had to go, much to her father's concern. He said no, and she said yes, and she won.

Kimberly flew first class to Iran with Lufthansa and was met at the airport in Tehran. The driver spoke no English and Kimberly spoke no Farsi. They arrived at the central hospital and Sam met Kimberly at the entrance. Kimberly was surprised that he wasn't sick. He gave her a give American hug and said, "I'm glad you are here. Now we are together for life."

Kimberly was shocked. For life? No. Her father was right. At her first opportunity, he sent a message to her father explaining the situation. She was totally surprised. Her father was as cool as a cucumber. All he said in a message was, "I'll take care of it."

Walter Baldwin called his former commanding officer by the name of Gen. Les Miller. Baldwin was also a general officer in the military. "Les, I have a problem. Can you help?"

General officers are a brand of their own. They take care of each other. General Baldwin explained the situation to General Miller. All the General said was, "We'll take care of it. We have experience dealing with those rascals. It'll take a few days. She'll be okay."

The general called Matt and explained the situation with Matt. He asked Matt to take care of the drone and he would ask Adam Benfield to give assistance, since he was Iranian and knew what to do.

"Adam, I have a job for you. You are still registered as a spy on Iran. Is that right?"

"I am," said Adam. "They send me a check every month. They do not expect anything from me. I told them I have HIV and they are deathly afraid of me. I still have all connections in Tehran waiting for me to come home. I know the drill General. How many people will be involved from your end?"

"I don't know yet." answered the General. "I'll check with Matt and Ashley. She will probably need a female escort."

The General got on his old military phone and contacted his old student friend Robert Peterson, the Iranian Vice President for whom he and Matt arranged the shipment of COVID vaccine that saved the country if Iran. Robert Peterson asked the General who the bad guy in Iran and the General said it was Sam Peterson."

Robert Peterson, the General's old school buddy answered, "He is my son. Sorry Les. You saved our country, and I'll take care of it on this end. We'll do an extraction on a holiday weekend."

Matt found that the special passenger drones were sitting idle in the drone base in Israel. He arranged for an passenger drone pilot that would be on call when the plans were worked. Without any incident whatsoever, Matt, Ashley, and the General were flown to the Israel drone base.

So, as it worked out, Matt, the General, and Ashley, were dressed in military uniforms. The General was a Four Star General, Matt was a Colonel, and Ashley was a Major. They flew to the abandoned

Iranian Sukhoi airfield in a drone, and were picked up by Adam Benfield in his Mercedes S500 and transported to a luxury hotel in Tehran. Benfield had flow to Iran by Lufthansa earlier. They were met at the hotel by Kimberly Baldwin and the Iranian vice present Robert Peterson. It was a happy meeting even though the people did not know each other. After a nice Iranian dinner, they have the world's best food – so they say, we steal it from everybody, the team slept in appropriate accommodations and were transported back to Sukhoi in a new Mercedes SUV. The drone to ride to Israel was without incident and they all, including Kimberly and Adam Benfield, were flown back to the states in the General's S550.

Don't Mess with Me

This is my story. Some people, and I am one of them, are so nice that people take advantage of them. We are not treated fairly, and the bad guys get away with it because the hurt people don't want to make a big fuss. Academics are the worst. This story is the exception.

It was an initial conference in a new field of study entitled Service Science. It was held at an appropriate university and was first rate as conferences go. I gave two papers that were appropriate by any standard and far exceeded any of the others. They were not in the proceedings with no good reason other than 'they weren't good enough.' The director was from some two-bit school in Canada. Well, I am a sophisticated person with a lot of books written, an enormous number of peer reviewed papers, and an outstanding amount of consulting at the highest level of organizations, such as the directors of the largest Swiss bank in addition to my professors duties. The conference was supported by a large computer company. They announced they were going to publish a journal on the new subject.

Within seconds, I conceptualized my response. Someone did not like my name, or my university, or something about which I have no knowledge. I carefully attended all of the sessions and introduced myself to the speaker. I complimented each and every one on a fine paper. I was on my way.

Back home at the ranch, not a real ranch, I contacted a friend who publishes journals and proposed a new journal on service science. He gave me a go and I said I would have the first issue in a month. I had twelve papers for issue #1 and twelve for issue #2. The publisher got the Library of Congress okay and we were go.

At that point, the supporting company had thousands of employees slotted for the new field and 500 research scientists worldwide.

I wanted to emphasize my accomplishment to the conference people and the company. I submitted a paper for their conference and got it accepted. I submitted my paper before my journal went live, so I was sure I had not violated anything.

They submitted their journal to the Library of Congress and the name had been taken. They didn't know what to do. Grown men.

The computer company supporting the new discipline got fed up with the management of it and cancelled the project. I won but I really didn't win in the long run. Something to think about.

It Happens Every Fall

After a couple of years teaching at the college level, you can predict what is going to happen on the first day of class. You discuss grade inflation, attendance, homework, and in computer classes, how to use the computer for students that are deadly afraid. You talk about eating in class and talking. Asking questions is always a good topic. You talk about the school's policy of dropping your lowest grade. And the genius that complained about the guy that got an F on a test and still got an A for the course.

We talk for some time on missing an exam, since I have the policy of giving make up exams. If you miss an exam, for any old reason, there is no reason to lie about it, I will give you a makeup exam. There is only one thing to think about. I give tests from a test bank that has several categories; easy, moderate, hard, difficult, and beyond belief. If you miss an exam, you get the next category exam. I'm reasonable about it, and in most semesters I rarely give at most one makeup. My policy is do what I tell you to do, and you do not have to worry about it. If the Ivy League can give grade inflation, so can I. Now to what this story is all about.

We have computers in all of the classrooms and you almost always have to hand in your work. In some cases, the printer is in another room. So when you do your work, put your name in the first line of the printed copy. You can always write your name on the top, but the printed line is the key.

You can always spot the athletes with a free ride. That means that tuition, books, room, board, and expenses are paid for. On the first day of class, they have a university cap and a pair of the latest Air Jordans, purchased at the bookstore. I never have found out how they do it but they do.

On the first day, an athlete turns a paper with his name written on the top, but someone else's name in the first line. Another stolen paper. Cheating. Kicked out of school. Lose athletic scholarship. Get 'ethics violation' on your transcript.

So you bring this up with the kid and he turns as white as snow. His life's dream of playing football is gone.

Then you lighten up and give him another chance. You can bet he never cheats again in all of his 4 years.

And of course, there is the A++ students mother, a professor at Yale, who calls every week to make sure her daughter is still getting an A. Life is good.

Ai

The question, "Can a machine think?" is one that has been debated for some time now and the question is no likely to be answered in this book. However, the subject is fruitful when considering "what a computer can do."

There are various opinions on the subject. Some say that thinking is an activity that is peculiar to human beings. Accordingly, machines cannot think. Although thought as something unique to humans may have been in the minds of early philosophers when they first considered the subject of thinking and intelligence, this does not really define the activity. Others maintain that a machine is thinking when it is performing activities that normally require thought when performed by human beings. Thus, adding 2+3 must be a form of thinking. To continue, some psychologists have defined have defined intelligence in the following simple way: intelligence is what an intelligence test measures. In light of the preceding section on information systems, all that needs to be done is to feed enough information into an information system and to develop an appropriate query language, and the result is an intelligent machine. This line of reasoning also skirts a clear definition. Perhaps, it is a waste of time to worry about precise definitions, but the fact remains that computers are doing some amazing things - such as playing chess, guiding robots, controlling space vehicles, recognizing patterns, proving theorems, and answering questions - and that these applications require much more than the conventional computer program. Richard Hamming, developer of the prestigious Hamming code for error detection and correction in computers, gives a definition of intelligent behavior that may be useful here:

The ability to act in subtle ways when presented with a class of situations that have not been exhaustively analyzed in advance, but which require rather different combinations of responses if the result in many specific cases is to be acceptable.

Artificial Intelligence is an important subject because it may indicate the direction in which society is moving. Currently, machines are used for two reasons: (1) The job cannot be done by a human being, and (2) The job can be performed more economically by a machine. To this list, another reason must be added: some jobs are simply too dull to be d one by humans, and it is desirable from a social point of view to have such jobs done by machine. This requires a greater number of "intelligent" machines, since people seem to be finding more and more work they consider to be dull and routine. Here are two items of interest before we get started with the talk:

Artificial general intelligence (AGI) is the intelligence of a machine that could successfully perform any intellectual task that a human being can. It is a primary goal of some AI research and is a common topic in science fiction and future studies. (Author unknown.)

The singularity is the hypothesis that the invention of artificial super intelligence (ASI) will abruptly trigger

runaway technical growth, resulting in unfathomable
change to human civilization. (Author unknown,)

It is possible to approach Artificial Intelligence from two points of view. Both approaches make use of programs and programming techniques. The first approach is to investigate the general principles of intelligence. The second is to study human thought, in particular.

Those persons engaged in the investigation of the principles of intelligence are normally charged with the development of systems that appear to be intelligent. This activity is commonly regarded as "artificial intelligence," which incorporates both engineering and computer science components.

Those same persons engaged in the study of human thought attempt to emulate human mental processes to a lesser or greater degree. This activity can be regarded as a form of "computer simulation," such that the elements of a relevant psychological theory are represented in a computer program. The objective of this approach is to generate psychological theories of human thought. The discipline is generally known as "Cognitive Science."

In reality, the differences between artificial intelligence and cognitive science tend to vary between "not so much" and "quite a lot" - depending upon the complexity of the underlying task. Most applications, as a matter of fact, contain elements from both approaches.

It is possible to zoom in on the scope of AI by focusing on the processes involved. At one extreme, the concentration is on the practicalities of doing AI programming, with an emphasis on symbolic programming languages and AI machines. In this context, AI can be regarded as a new way of doing programming. It necessarily follows that hardware/software systems with AI components have the potential for enhanced end-user effectiveness.

At the other extreme, AI could be regarded as the study of intelligent computation. This is a more grandiose and encompassing focus with the objective of building a systematic and encompassing focus with the objective of building a systematic theory of intellectual processes - regardless if they model human thought or not.

It would appear, therefore, that AI is more concerned with intelligence in general and less involved with human thought in particular. Thus, it may be contended that humans and computers are simply two options in the genus of information processing systems.

Just in Case – The Window

Well, just in case you are sick and tired with all of this doing, not doing, going, not going, remembering and not remembering, and want to just sit back and enjoy the day, here is something kind of fun for you. You can copy it if you want to:

The Window

Now why would anyone write about one of the most common things in the modern world: a window. After all, there are windows all over the place, and many of them don't have anything covering them up. Probably, there is an interest in windows – especially open ones – because there is almost always a sort of mystery associated with a window. There is natural inclination to find out what's going on. Is it something new and challenging, is it something drastic, is it something that is exceedingly happy or terribly sad?

Try to conceptualize strolling in the country side and coming upon an older building with blown out open windows, what is the first thing you think? Probably it is that no one cares. But that is not necessarily true. Perhaps the owner has passed away and just does not know that the beloved structure with damaged windows is in need of repair. Does caring end with death? Well, that is an open item. It seems that life in the modern world is nothing more than an ever expanding set of open items. Back to the wide world of windows.

It is entirely possible that there were never any covers of any kind over the rectangular "holes in a proverbial wall". The place was simply not finished, a commonplace consequence for a variety of everyday reasons. What about the windows in some of those middle-eastern homes. It seems as though they typically don't have anything covering the windows – at least that's how they are portrayed in the daily news. Probably it is easier to shoot through an open window and even an open door. That pertains to inside out and is likely true of outside in.

Modern office buildings are frequently designed to be window friendly and look like walls of glass. Obviously there are supporting structures placed in strategic locations to support the whole thing. They are certainly hot in summer and cold in winter giving a lot of work for heating and air conditioning people and also window washers, in addition to window covers and stuff like that.

A thing that some people apparently do is look into other people's windows to see what is going on.

The first assumption made in this case is that the objective is to look at the people in hope of seeing something juicy. But how juicy can it really be? Probably, the objective for a good number of inside lookers – called peeping toms – is simply to see how the decorations look. Illegal activity is another thing that is too complicated for words.

Now looking out of a window could also be pretty interesting since windows are up a bit and a person can see farther out. So that brings up an unusual question. Why don't artistic painters depict scenes from a raised position? Of course, some do but not many. Practically everything that one could think of has been done – somewhere in the vast world – even painting a window scape.

There are many additional sorts of windows, many of them. What about the windows associated with computers. An electronic display device is used for input and output on most modern computers, as well as tablets and smart phones. In fact, it is common to see windows inside of windows, and so forth. Millions of dollars are regularly spent by electrical engineers designing display technology enabling windows to be brighter and more readable. Practically everyone knows these days that a piece of software called an operating system is needed to use a computer and that includes phones and tablets, including music players and games. There is a major one called Windows produced by the Microsoft Corporation and the name is trademarked.

Motor vehicles have windows to see out of. The main window is called the windshield that also blocks the wind when moving. Some early cars and trucks did not have wind shields and the driver and front passenger had to wear goggles, much like airplane pilots. In vehicles, there are also side windows, a rear window, and a top window sometimes referred to as a sun roof or a moon roof. Usually the top roof opens for added pleasure. Lately, it has become common to have the top roof cover the entire roof. It is called a panoramic roof. Here is an amazing observation. It is commonplace, especially in Florida and California, to see people riding along the motor ways with the top down. Do you remember seeing someone riding along with the sun roof open?

Have you been downtown lately? Maybe not, but major retail stores have splashy windows, usually around holidays. The main idea is to put people into the holiday mood so they come and buy stuff that they probably do not need to buy, at least at the moment. It seems as though, however, that it is a bit more than that. It's a competition. Which store has the best windows? In this instance, it is not the window, per se, but what is displayed behind the window. Typically, the store will feature pleasing and esthetically appropriate items to showcase. There are even businesses that will prepare windows for a fee, but the pleasure is often in the doing in addition to the result.

Have you ever ridden in an airplane? If you have, then you can guess what this paragraph is going to be all about. If you're lucky, you had the experience of flying in a private jet. Most people say it is pure pleasure. But why? You will soon find out. In the past, commercial air travel was a pleasure. You checked your luggage at the curb and proceeded forthwith to check in at the counter. The passenger space was ample and a meal was usually served if flight time permitted it. If you were fortunate enough to travel first class, you enjoyed orange juice or champagne when you got to your seat that was also first class. During flight, it used to be interesting to look out to see what is going on, and the seats and windows were aligned to facilitate this form of activity. Well, those days are long gone. In order to maximize revenue, airlines have stuffed many seats into a space that was limited to start with, so that a real window is unlikely. Airplane builders have come up with a new kind of window; a window that is not a window, but a computer screen showing an outside scene. The seats and windows are still not aligned, but passengers do not care after they go through check in.

Harry Katzan Jr.

Welcome to "Windows of the World". You've undoubtedly seen a sign like that, somewhere in this vast country. As mentioned, if you can think it, then it probably exists. Scenic attractions commonly view their services as a window to something fun, enjoyable, and worthy of your attention. A good book is a window to whatever the book contains. Hundreds of "Windows to ..." can easily be imagined.

An interval of time can also be regarded as a window, as in "You have a time window of three days to get to the west coast". Almost anything that is time dependent can be expressed in terms of a window. Moreover, anything you can see through is a window, even though it may be on the floor or the ceiling. Most windows are rectangular, although some are round, square, and all sorts of shape.

So just what is the window and just what is the something that is not a window. A window has been defined as an opening in a wall to allow light, air, or just about anything else to get in. If you break a hole in the side of a barn that allows in light, air, dust, and all manners of bugs, have you created a window? Most people would class that as a nasty hole in the wall. Not a window. Many people say that anything you can see through is a window, even though it may be on the floor or the ceiling. Most windows are rectangular, although some are round, square, and all sorts of shape. To finish the definition of a window, it is an opening with casements or sashes that contain transparent material, such as glass or plastic, capable of being open or closed. A glass window that can't be opened and an opaque window are still windows. Some windows are classed by what they do for people. But a window, per se, does not really do anything. It just sits there, looking kind of stupid. A ticket window is used to distribute tickets, so to speak, to customers who use the same facility to obtain them. But, isn't that exactly what most things in the world do. They kind of sit there looking kind of stupid for other people to use.

It's getting a little cool in here so I'll close the window.

Just in Case – A Smile

Well, just in case you are still sick and tired with all of this not doing, doing, not going, going, not remembering and remembering, and want to just lie down and enjoy the day, here is something else kind of fun for you. You can copy it if you want to:

A Smile

I was heading down Atlantic Avenue in Boston to the office building where I work. It was noontime and the sidewalk was filled with people. As I walked, I was eating a candy bar. I don't even remember why and what kind it was. I approached a nice looking young women, who had a huge smile on her face. At the time I thought the smile was because of the candy bar that I was eating. The smile started at a distance and lasted until we passed each other. I have a lingering memory of that event. It made me feel good – a simple smile. What was it about a smile that would make a person – namely me - remember the episode? What is a smile anyway?

A smile is a facial expression accomplished by opening one's mouth slightly or minimally showing the teeth and flexing the lips. A smile may be seen in the twinkle of the eyes. In the latter case it is called a 'Dushine' smile. The word 'smial' is derived from the middle English word 'smilen.' There a lot of sayings that include the word smile, such as people commonly say, "Smile and people smile with you; frown and you frown alone." Actually, there are two forms if the word smile. There is the noun representing the smile itself, and the verb form that is the act of smiling and called the aforementioned Dushine smile. There are two substitutes for the word smile: beam and grin. For example, the boy received a bicycle for Christmas and he was beaming. Alternately, the word grin is more common, as in George has a foolish grin on his face after telling a joke.

Do all people smile? Probably not. You rarely see a farmer or industrial worker smile. Did Galileo, Plato, or Aristotle smile? We don't know and probably never will. My guess is that they did not smile very much if at all, because life was tough in those days, so a smile would certainly be regarded as a sign of weakness. Perhaps, that is true today, but I doubt it.

Girls smile a lot – or should I say women. Clearly, it seems as though they would wish people to like them.

Now, here is an interesting case. Some speakers on TV in the modern world smile between sentences.

Harry Katzan Jr.

It works. They are in fact more effective than those who do not. Also, smiles sell toothpaste.

Can a smile be a sign of aggression? Yes, and no. Usually not. A smile is usually a sign of friendship. But in gangster and western movie, a toothy smile is a sign of, "I don't like you." Do football coaches on the sidelines smile? I wonder.

Lately, people have been wearing face masks to protect against a virus. Can you detect a smile behind the mask? Some people say they can, you can always rely on the twinkle of an eye. Here is a smiley story. I was walking down the hallway at the university and came upon a student basketball player. Being behind the times in that regard, I asked him what a point guard was. He smiled with a big grin and told me. We came upon some other students and they were also smiling as big as life. The traditional roles of teacher- student were reversed. Now that is a real reason to smile.

My goal is to make someone happy every day. So I'm going to finish now and find someone to smile at.

Author: Harry Katzan, Jr.

END OF STORY FIFTY TWO

Harry Katzan Jr.

Harry Katzan Jr.

ABOUT THE AUTHOR

Harry Katzan, Jr. is a professor who has written several books and many papers on computers and service, in addition to some novels. He has been an advisor to the executive board of a major bank and a general consultant on various disciplines. He and his wife have lived in Switzerland where he was a banking consultant and a visiting professor. He is an avid runner and has completed 94 marathons including Boston 13 times and New York 14 times. He holds bachelors, masters, and doctorate degrees.

SOME NOVELS BY HARRY KATZAN, JR.

The Mysterious Case of the Royal Baby

The Curious Case of the Royal Marriage

A Case of Espionage

Shelter in Place

Life is Good

A Tale of Discovery

The Terrorist Plot

An Untimely Situation

The Final Escape

The Day After The Night Before

Retired Old Men Eating Out, Vol. 1

Retired Old Men Eating Out. Vol 2

The Last Adventure

Lessons in Artificial Intelligence

On the Trail of Artificial Intelligence

Printed in the United States
by Baker & Taylor Publisher Services